The Mickey

Full House

Corbet's Couloir

Eat a Peach

Home Sweet Home

The Waiting

Ramschackled

Thankful

Boys Club Full House

Slowly moving off the couch he felt uneasy at first but Mickey knew it was the right thing to do even if his spirit was down, neglected and in need of repair. He had hung on the couch until 11am and watching TV movies until he found his tennis shoes. It was a short walk to the best espresso latte' in town where Garcia would smile at him while speaking Spanish to the other barista. Feeling lucky, he grabbed the last

New York Times off the stand and retreated back to the Holiday House. Grumbling back to the pad, thinking about all the work he wasn't doing, he determined that he was being unbearable to even himself. He walked up the steps with a hot coffee and fresh paper in hand. There was something about the New York Times that drifted nostalgia, reminding him of Sunday mornings after church and his father.

Dutch came home for lunch and was struck with the amount of negativity on the couch and the pile of dishes by the sink. "You're killing me here man. No, no, you're killing yourself. Is any woman worth this self-loathing gutter you are in? Think about it man". There was no response from the couch. Mickey's attention drifted back to the Times and his now cold coffee. From the kitchen could be heard the sounds of a man on his lunch break doing another man's dishes.

When the water stopped running, Dutch came out with a towel on his shoulder and one in his hand drying a plate. "That's it! You are going to Jackson with us next week. So start getting some airfare together. The beds are all taken so you are on the couch, but you are coming man, you got that!" It was not a question and Mickey didn't respond anyway but rather nodded and said something about talking later. "Won't be such a big change for you anyway, seeing as you are on the couch most of the time around here anyway. So get your skis tuned down at Cal Ski, because you are going to be skiing with the big boys. You might get some better ski pants and some long underwear 'cause you know how cold it can get up there".

The Holiday House was a California Craftsman style with character drenched hardwood
floors and had built in bookshelves and redwood walls that ran up to molding with white walls above. You could breathe in the wondrous flavor of Julia Morgan designs that were popularly built at the time. Their only down side was that they were dark, especially in the winter after the time got set back. When the sun dropped below the Live Oaks at midday it made for even more darkness. And it was this darkness which finally slapped Mickey out of his funk and off the couch.

He decided he needed another one but planned to drink it up at The French. Mickey didn't always drink coffee in the afternoon but thought it might blast him out of his dark outlook and hoped the buzz would straighten him out. He was surprised to find that it was actually a fairly nice day out and it was warmer outside than inside the cave of their living room. By the time he got up to the Ave it was sunny and he had to reach for his sunglasses. Rounding the corner he entered the northern stretch of the Gourmet Ghetto, known for intelligent food preparation in kitchens that used organic and naturally grown, locally sustainable agriculture. He could smell the coffee, now only a little bit north of the hotel. "No foam Cap" he ordered. Garcia was still there and talking to his partner. Mickey grabbed his cup and a Madeline and sat down at a bistro table outside with the section of the New York Times that he hadn't finished.

That first sip of coffee brought an "Ahhh" which is always a sign of a good cup. He reflected on what Dutch had said. Perhaps he was right. It wasn't exactly a question and Mickey decided to just do it, shake things up and maybe it would be just the thing. Sitting outside was almost hot as he was in the direct sun, catching just an edge of it at the front of The French, and it warmed him. He thought for a moment about Jackson and what Dutch had said about it being cold and almost got shiver thinking about it. But he really didn't know how cold it can get up there in January and had only heard stories of winds cresting at fifty miles an hour in the thirty below temps. He had only been there in the summer time, in August, on a backpacking trip.

Jackson Hole, Wyoming in the wintertime is a Mecca for snow riders of all sorts these days. But the year was 1986 and there were no snowboards except for the hybrid boards being created up at Donner Ski Ranch in California. Ex-surfers and radical skate boarder types were pushing the limits of traditional snow sports, anxious to apply their side standing talents to the snow. Currently one can find skate-skiers, snowboarders, kite-skiers, mountaineering Nordic skiers with lock down heels and of course skiers, up on the slopes.

But these were simpler times in the ski world. Mickey had been photographed on a pair of wood skis at age four although there had been huge gaps in his ski world. High school friends got him back into it however that was a long time ago and he wasn't very good. Control was not an attribute easily applied to him. It was really more about following the girls. He skied briefly in Colorado during his college days but had just recently gotten back into the sport being encouraged by his friend in Berkeley. It was this friend, Dutch, with whom a new adventure would begin.

Two weeks ago he'd broken up with yet another woman. Mickey was recovering from a relationship gone bad and being the sensitive sort, this affected him. Dutch, seeing him down had told him he had to go, for his own sanity if not for that of his roommate. There was simply no peace in the barnyard. Their usual carefree had shifted to the glum and morose and this was something that couldn't be tolerated at the Berkeley pad, otherwise known as the Holiday House.

In the next week or so, Mickey pulled some things together with work and arranged his travel out to Wyoming. In particular, he pulled himself together, wrenching himself off the womb of the couch and greeting the day in the early morning like he usually did. He was on a countdown to getting out of town and that in itself, cheered him.

And as things were slow, and he had just finished a big project, planning a trip worked well. He would have to travel alone, as everyone else was on a package special that included airfare. Mickey didn't mind this though, and even enjoyed being the loner. It allowed him to be anonymous.

Getting out of town usually has its cravats and upheaval but seeing as he had no life, as in no work and no girlfriend, it was easy. He slid right into it, making it to the airport with plenty of time to spare. It was raining when he left and that was always a good sign for a ski trip. The weather comes in from the West and rolls across the western states, landing at the ski resorts. At least that's the way it's supposed to work. He was keeping his eye on the rain up in Washington and western Canada, for it is that precipitation that makes it to northwestern Wyoming.

At the time there were no direct flights to Jackson Hole from most places and no large aircraft came into the undersized airport. So it was with trepidation that he boarded a twenty passenger prop plane that would make the short hop from Salt Lake City. He seated himself by a window, hoping to see the peaks as they went. With great commotion a Hispanic family was boarding just as he got seated. The man, in a distinguished dark suit with a grey shirt and no tie, was carrying the children's bags and the three kids were between himself and his wife who was bringing up the rear. Crouching to get a better look out the windows and onto the wings he motioned to the flight attendant in a nervous manner and asked in a thick South American accent "Miss, where are the jets engines?" Suzy, her bright nametag read on top of her blue blazer and brightly stripped shirt. "Yes sir, no these are propellers, this is a prop-plane." Looking at her as if he had never heard of such a thing he emphatically questioned this. "No Jets? There are no jets engines on this plane?" He didn't wait for her to finish her negative response, instead turning to his wife, shouting now "Maria, get the childrens – we are leavings – there are no jets engines on these plane. Maria, grab the children, we must go now!" The family of five did a turnaround in the small aisle and Mickey couldn't help but notice the urgency of his shouted orders. He wondered if they knew something he did not. When they were off the plane, he shuffled in his seat and looked around to see only three other passengers. They looked like businessmen and they didn't look up from their reports and newspapers. He got Suzy's attention and ordered a double Bloody Mary which he had in his hand before the plane took off.

On the ground, Mickey at once felt relieved and content. Stepping off the plane, down the stairs the ground crew had rolled out to the plane, was a slap in the face. The air was beyond crisp and was punishing as he was in a thin pair of Bay Area Levi jeans that offered no protection against the cold. He was shivering by the time the hundred and fifty foot walk from the planes resting place on the tarmac was over and relieved to feel the heat inside. A six foot guy in a cowboy hat greeted him with a "howdy" and Mickey knew he wasn't in California anymore.

Arriving at the resort and walking under a covered area, he came out by the bar to see the expanse of the mountain in front of him. The sun had gone down a few minutes ago and the sunset was bold and tremendous. He could see the groomer machines up on the hill already, getting a start on a long night of working the slopes. Resting his skies and backpack by a lodge pole pine column, he couldn't help feel the profound beauty here.

Standing there in front of the Moose Bar that day, he got the feeling that this was something special. There was a magic about this place and a serene beauty that filled the soul like the crisp mountain air at eleven thousand feet.

The cold ceased to bother him as he just starred at the mountain trails that wound down from a peak that couldn't be seen, lost in the clouds. After some time, all he could really see was the lights on the groomers so, leaving his bags he ventured into the Moose for an Irish coffee and some directions. There was no worry about someone stealing anything, not here in this pristine beauty.

With little effort he located the condo after walking with his gear thru the parking lot and then up one of the adjoining roads. Although they had gotten in hours earlier, it was too late to ski that day. Coming up on #12 he didn't knock, but just opened the door, which was of course unlocked. In the entry were everyone's skis, nestled between pine pegs to get them standing properly. Mickey gave out a "Hey" and as he rounded the corner towards the kitchen, about six "heys" came back and with that he felt right at home. Taking off his jacket as the heat had been cranked up, he went around saying hello to everyone giving a high five to Dutch first.

The poker game had already begun. Mickey hadn't played a lot but admired the game. These guys looked like they were players. Grabbing a beer out of the fridge he came over to the table and again offered a "hey", but more of a group greeting this time. "Pull up a seat Mickey" and he did so, reaching for his wallet as he sat down.

Deciding to ease into it was a good decision. His idea was to get the lay of the land and get to know these guys a bit and find out how they played. On top of that, he wasn't that good playing poker and hadn't gambled too much before. And then there were the wild cards. Mickey hated wild cards and thought they created a different game, not necessarily bad, just not poker. But he was trying to be flexible.

The deal was passed around clockwise and it seemed to be quarter bets, so how bad could he get dinged, he thought. But the pace was furious and the pots got bigger than he would have thought for quarters and the pots were large by his standards. With the raising and raising they got up to twenty dollars. This seemed exorbitant but he played along. He got up a few times and had some food but the game always was on. Dutch said they started when they first entered the townhouse. Mickey was in for the ante put that was about it.

Suddenly he was dealt a queen and king and was in for the flop. He raised the bet a buck but remained stoic. John looked at him in amazement retorting "I was wondering when you were going to start playing poker." Mickey produced a large gleam even if this wasn't his poker face. "Well maybe I finally got some decent cards". John just rolled his head side to side and re-raised laughing a bit and said "and maybe you don't have anything." Mickey bought into the fury with another raise which everyone agreed was the third and last one. The flop came up with two kings and a jack. The only problem Mickey counseled his inner voice, was that there were three hearts showing. There was a pretty healthy round of betting and raises but there were still two more cards to come. The next card turned a four of hearts and everyone starred at was obviously the flush to come. Four straight hearts sat up pretty and the table stirred with the excitement. The excitement of Mickey's three of a kind dimmed with the advent of this new heart but he continued with the betting because he couldn't walk away from three of a kind. The river card produced a queen of clubs which delighted Mickey but he tried to keep his optimism in check. A full house and a slew of flush dogs on the table, he thought. What better situation could a poker player ask for?

And there it was. The best friend of a full house is the guy that can't hide his glee behind a flush. There were five players still in and Mickey figured at least four of them were holding a heart. Maybe one of them had three of a kind, but when you are starring at four hearts in Texas Hold-em there is little doubt that at least one held the flush. If you are sitting there with three of a kind you would be concerned at this point. If someone else had a full boat, it would have to beat kings. Mickey didn't have to look at his down cards and instead studied the looks from across the table. And as the dealer was to his right his was the first bet and he decided to slow play it to check the barometer at the table.

The first player to his left, Rein, a tall slim Estonian, went in for the maximum table bet of two dollars. The next player, Bobby, called and the bet was two dollars to Little Napoleon. They called him that for his autocratic way of running his business. Bobby worked for him, but never called that to his face and then only with reserved tone. LN, as he was most often called, was astonished at the bet. "Four buckolas to me huh? Man, that's getting stiff isn't it?" There was a few moments of silence as he considered his flush and Mickey wondered who had the highest heart in their hand. "alright, I'm in" was the retort as he threw in his four dollars. Dutch didn't have a grin on his broad cheeks. His lips were pursed and he rubbed the end of his chin nervously for longer than normal, not hearing any of the chatter at the table. "I'll raise. That's four bucks to you Mickey." Mickey took his time as if he had something to consider. After the appropriate amount of consideration Mickey reached for his wallet saying "I'll raise" The table erupted with shouts about the rules. "No that's already three raise bets and that's the max" said LN who only called the bet. "No way cried Bobby "I didn't raise, I just called, so it's four bucks to Mickey" After consternation and chaos settled into silence, Mickey said " Okay then, I guess I'll just have to raise it one more time" and he put his six bucks in with bravado. Dutch asserted himself as the dealer and pointing to each player, said "so that's four to Rein and Bobby, four bucks to LN and two to me." Having seen everyone throw in their worn dollar bills he directed everyone to "show 'em." Mickey was unsure about going first but catching a nod from Dutch, he threw down his king and queen on top of the money. The table erupted in litany of moans, groans and poor language. It was not surprising to Mickey that no one showed their cards but he knew they had flush cards and there might have been a straight in there as well as that jack on the flop got involved.

Mickey hauled in his seventy-five dollar pot. He was top dog for that hand but didn't get too much else that night. He was glad to walk away from the table with at least sixty dollars and figured he had just bought his ski pass for tomorrow. The game lingered on until at least eleven when everyone made their way to their bedrooms. The couch did Mickey fine and he went to bed with a smile on his lips, thinking about those kings and queens.

Corbet's Couloir

There we two skiers at the entrance and Mickey wondered if they were going to jump in, but they were just there for a look too. After some of the boys took a look Mickey sidestepped over to the three or four foot wide entrance, surrounded by tall snow on either side. It was really just a notch in the snow wall. He gingerly got as close to the edge has he dared and peeking over gasped out a "damn" and turning towards Dutch a "whooaa." His left leg twitched a little bit as he looked down the chute and he didn't want to get any closer. It was a least a ten foot vertical drop into the chute. "Once you are in there it is just three quick turns and you are in the good stuff at the bottom" offered Dutch as he squeezed in for a look. There were menacing rocks on either side of the top of the chute which was only six or seven feet wide. Those three quick turns would have to be that indeed, Mickey thought as they skied down the ridge where the boys were gathered.

"Let's ski down to Thunder and do a warm up run guys" said LN and they all followed together into the Rendezvous Bowl and to the left on a trail name Gros Ventre which went through the top of Laramie Bowl. Mickey decided to stay on Gros Ventre while everyone else jumped into the black diamond run called Thunder. Both runs came out at the Thunder chair but they blew by this and went all the way to the bottom on Gros Ventre.

Tom was the tram guide. He was sublime in his coolness, all dark and handsome in his demeanor. He wore the official jackets with the Hole logo. Once the doors were closed and the gate was sealed they were welcomed by their guide. "Welcome to European skiing in the Western United States. Please be advised that this is not a beginner tram and that there are no green runs from top. Our trip to the top will be a short twelve minutes and will rise almost two miles to the top of Rendezvous Mountain ………."

Mickey kept his gaze on the village as long as he could and then with his head turning slowly towards his right as he breathed in the mountain. Cruising at a good pace now the tram plied its way upwards, staying in the forest line and following the bottom of Gros Ventre. Going thru the woods above the pines they rode until they breached tree line and the mountain revealed itself.

After passing overhead of the Riverton Bowl and over the Thunder Run the landscape dropped below and there was a great deal of distance to the tram in the air. This part of the mountain offered the highest elevation of the tram where you looked downwards quite a distance. You passed over cliffs that were out of bounds and over the East Ridge Traverse where that distance was either greater or seemed so because of the terrain. This was the point where Corbet's Couloir came most sharply into focus as it was right up the mountain.

As Mickey was looking at the entrance he could see a skier in the "go" position with his ski tips hanging off the edge. "Wicked" he said to himself but out loud and his vision went macro, narrowing in on the fogged up window. Just at that moment, the door sprung open with no warning or reason and he found himself two inches to the edge of moving tram car. It rolled along as normal ridding above ridges and chutes and tops of trees. Sixty-five people issued a collective sigh in a high pitch. It was more of a yelp by people scared to death. The wind blew the fourteen degree shards into his face as the shocked tram car retracted from the two doors on either side. "Oh my GOD" shouted a women in a thick Brooklyn accent as she clung to her husband. She kept saying it like a mantra but it was becoming annoying.

Mickey was standing there not moving at all, not frozen but being purposely slow keeping his head on a swivel. Time slowed down. The panorama of the mountain flowing out the open doors was enticingly vivid, not being filtered thru the tram door window. It was, however stark and cold and he knew he was alive. Everyone else had sucked into the center and

Mickey alone was still by the door, afraid to let go of the handle rail he had found. He had not yet looked down at his ski boots terse at the thought of seeing how close he was to edge. So he kept his gaze level with the horizon but looking to each side with regular motions. He had noticed how slippery his plastic ski boots were on the frozen snow that laced the steel and was not inclined to test his steadiness and so didn't move a centimeter.

"Base! Base this is car one. Our doors just popped open and we are still moving. Base this is car one can you advise." They could all hear the tension in his voice, not at all confident and cocky like before.

"Rodger that. Bill is up top and we are monitoring you on the grid. Our suggestion is to ride it to the top"

Repeating this he cupped his hands over the speaker to keep the volume down and not contribute to the obvious anxiety. The car was packed in tightly filling up the middle of the car. Some were able to move towards the ends but most could make little progress. Everyone with the clunky ski boots, they were a thundering herd of turtles. The hard plastic base of the ski boots slid around quite well on the galvanized steel floor. The addition of moisture and some snow made it slippery indeed. Some, trying to move away from the two yard width of sure death had turned at angles and many had their backs to the opening. Some of these folks had the worst of it.

"One, do you have a pulse on the DRS? Is that normal or are you having any other issues?"

When the sixty five riders are loaded into the tram car there is a natural shuffling for personal space. The window towards the front is the favorite with everyone heading directly there for a first class view. But as the car fills, the middle area gets filled up last and there are fewer bars to grab onto for balance. In the Tokyo subways there are paid "people pushers" that force more people into the subways, knowing that there is always a little more room inside. The ski guides do the same thing somewhat, although they have an accurate count which is mandated for safety. It's just human nature to mark your area and define it by your ski boot and ski footprint. But on this day, here on this car, they found room themselves pulling together and being a team. Like oxygen being sucked out of hermetically sealed container, the snow riders sucked it in and no one wanted to be near the door. With the doors wide open on either side, that first step was a big one, over a thousand feet straight down to a craggy rock death. Everyone had done their part, moving the boulder ski boots inch by inch until there was three feet in front of each door.

"Mickey! Mickey!" Dutch yelled to get his attention. Mickey hadn't moved from his position by the door. He had tried to move backwards but ran into the guy behind him and almost lost his balance. So, in desperation, he was trying to just maintain his balance which he was doing fairly well. However the tram was still moving up the hill and the wind was slicing into one door and out the other. In the micro system of his two feet by the door, Mickey failed to realize that the tram was approaching the number three tower, the last below the cliffs at the top of Rendezvous. Even on a windless day on the mountain, when the tram passes a tower it naturally does a dip forward and then compensates with a backward tilt until it levels off. Mickey was unaware of the approaching tower and was afraid to look around, trying to keep steady with his right hand braced against the inside of the door jam. "Mickey!" Dutch yelled again and this time he heard it but still he was stuck in his indecisiveness. His mind was racing in a whirl of inaction as they came right up on the tower and with the forward dip beginning. With his ski boots two inches from the edge his steadiness waned just as felt the large hand of Dutch grab the back of his hood. Reaching between the heads of two women he said like a leader "I've Gotcha now, just back up a little bit more dude. That's it- let's make a little space for him people That's it. We're good here. Everybody just stick together. We're almost to the top."

With the forward dip, three women in the front had screamed in unison and a German couple were fluidly engaged in what seemed like an argument. The Tram slowed up now as it approached the platform which brought about another sway forward and a slight one back.

The Tram Car rolled into the barn at its usual slow down pace, having passed the entrance tower. They came in as normal and Mickey noticed the gates were opened, not closed as usual. All the ski patrol guys that were up top were there in a line, with a paramedic and rescue guy. Mickey jumped off first. He was pulled by a number of fists until he was at the back where an excited rescue dog came over and gave him a lick on his hand, checking him in his own way. Convinced that Mickey was fine he turned around to check on the others

One by one the crew showed up over to the left side where they had met before. Rein and LN and Bobby and the glory became their own. A huge boisterous "waahooo" came with the high fives. "Mickey, I can't believe how long you hung out there dude. Seriously dude I guess you had a comfort zone there but it was driving me crazy. You were hanging ten. Man, I'm going to call you Hangten from now on dude. Hangten" Mickey would remark years later, that he had never, since that day, called him Hangten.

They headed down the traverse and Mickey, who was out in front, skied right over to the Corbett's entrance. There was no one at the opening now and Mickey skied right up and climbed to the top where he hung his tips the way he had seen it done. After a minute looking down he thought that this didn't seem like anything after the tram ride. But reasoning the better, he turned around and headed down the trail.

Mickey decided to let the big dogs bark over on the Hoback Ridge and nurtured his skills on some gentler runs. The system at Jackson is askew he thought, after skiing down a run marked not with the black diamond (most difficult) or the blue (moderately difficult) but there was this new red (most difficult). He had never seen this break down but thought the blue was like a black diamond anywhere else. He plied his skis to Sleeping Indian and Wide Open and worked on his turns. He stayed at it all day, feeling comfortable over there and glad not to be on the top of the mountain.

Eat a Peach

The next morning Mickey had to get up early. On Saturdays he did a special job for his friends who owned an organic peach farm about seventy miles east of San Francisco. Mickey didn't do early. But he hated being late and always tried to be where he was supposed to be. He used to say that the latest he had ever arrived was on time. But that record was in peril as he careened across the Bay Bridge on a western approach pattern to Ferry Building near the Clock Tower for the weekly Organic Farmer's Market. The San Francisco icon where 1906 earthquake survivors gathered for a boat ride across the bay to Oakland and Berkeley was now home to the foodies who gathered weekly for organic produce, crafted delights and fresh caught salmon from the chilly waters off the coast.

There was a certain glow down by the bay on those warm summer mornings. Looking east across the San Francisco Bay, the low sun hung close to the horizon at 6:45am. It would heat up by noon but it was always crisp on the bay when the sun came up. It was quiet also. Odd to be so quiet here in the middle of a major metropolitan area. Most of the people on the streets had something to do with the farmers market. There was your usual jogger presence and a few homeless souls. But street people knew better that to be in this part of town right now. They wandered down for the view and some panhandling in the afternoon, but not in the morning. There were warmer places a few blocks away out of the breeze or by an office building's heating vent. Even though it was the heart of the summer, the nights and mornings were cold, especially in the shade.

Waking up to his Peet's Coffee took more than one cup this morning. He went in and got one of Becky's famous baked goods and large mug of Peet's. Although he hated getting up at 5:30, once he was here, in the quiet, there was serenity. The Seagull's symphony was a theme song in the background. Their shrill commentary about their breakfast favored chaos by its nature, the sounds came thru to Mickey that morning like a Zen mantra that focused him totally on his coffee, his baked good and the unlikely harmony of nature in the heart of a city. So, he pulled himself off the jogger's path and took a moment. The light before 7am is like no other. The horizon was three-dimensional in its clarity and the water picked up the cobalt blue of the sky. The water was like glass. Not a ripple to be seen except for an occasional sea lion flipper.

Just then a guy that lived in his motorized wheelchair came buzzing by about twenty five miles an hour. He was wearing three sweaters but they all had the same color of dirt. His beard was long and shaggy and he gazed straight ahead as he went forward. The whirling sound made the Seagulls scream and flee. Mickey thought of doing the same. The moment was lost.

"Well, better get up and get to work" he thought, taking a long pull on the French Roast and a deep long inhale of the rare early morning air being warm and then into the madness of the farmer's market. Like a roaming band of Indigenous Americans setting up teepees they came from all points, except west of course. The flower guy was from Moss Landing. The Salmon guy came up from Santa Cruz. There was the Cowgirl Creamery from Point Reyes and vegetables came for further points east, soaking up the full frontal sun shots in the fertile delta. They came, set up their encampments and at the end of the day they broke camp leaving little sign that they were even there. The tent city that welcomed thousands throughout the day with their bags and carts, was returned to its regular bay side form.

The first job was setting up the tent. When he arrived at their spot, Becky was wrestling the tent by her lonesome. Her arms were spread eagle holding the top piece with her right hand and trying to push the little button and bring down the tin legs. Mickey jumped right in, grabbing the other pole and jacking it. Within a minute, they had their structure up, tables aligned that featured selling the baked goods and jams. They had defined their parameters and set up their territory. They didn't want to be too close to the chicken guy – a large Ford Econoline with a giant chicken head on the top of the roof. At the end of the day they would get a free roasted chicken if they had any left, so being neighborly was important. But smelling chicken all day makes you not want chicken for a few days, so your exact placement was important and made the day work.

Mickey once had a job in high school at a restaurant. He had to make up a five gallon container of Blue Cheese Salad Dressing, working it with a large spoon. After doing this for a summer, Mickey couldn't eat Blue Cheese for about fifteen years without getting a gag reflex. He didn't want this to happen with chickens.

As Becky went back and forth between the inside shop and our tent outside the Clock Tower, he began setting up the grill. A large commercial gas grill, it was five feet long and about two deep. Becky and Farmer Al had come over for dinner last fall and dinner for Mickey meant barbeque. They called him the Patio Daddio and whenever he was at someone's party or was invited over for dinner he wound up at the grill. It was his thing.

"Peaches? We're going to grill peaches" he asked over the phone. "Yeah. With Pancetta". "I'm not totally sure I know what that is, but it sound delicious" The idea was not Becky's but came from head chef at a local restaurant on Nob Hill called Quinces. It was instantly hailed as a success. Becky got word and from there put together a new tent with that was all about grilled peaches wrapped in Pancetta.

The first week Becky got him a case of peaches and big bundle of pancetta, saying he should experiment. It turned out that the secret was to cook them hard, getting the pancetta nice and crispy and then put them off to the side so the sugars in the peach would crystallize, sitting there on the back burner. If you cooked them too fast the outside would be too crispy and the peach juices not sweet enough. If you don't cook them hard and fast then the pancetta would be soft and fatty looking. It was still good but didn't the cosmetic quality that people craved.

Toddy and Mickey got in the groove about nine am when the crowds would gather and a line would form. Like a hawker at a carnival they hollered "Get your grilled Frog Hollow Peaches wrapped in Hobbs Pancetta". Sometimes, they added that they were "grilled with love and tasted like it!" Sometimes the Giants fans would stop by on the way to the ballpark and the boys would holler "San Francisco Giants Grilled Peaches with Pancetta! Can't get 'em inside the park so get 'em now!" Toddy had developed his own tune and sang it like with a melody: "Grilled Peaches: we got em – you'll love em", "Get your San Francisco Grilled Frog Hollow………."

It became an art form- a theatrical presentation of street theater and art. Define art. James Joyce defined it as not the art itself that was important, but the way you did it. It was the way you lived your life and what you got out of it. That pretty much summed up Mickey's life today. He was making peaches and pancetta as art.

There was one guy that was always the first customer at 8am. He said that he began his day thinking about them. He had his coffee on his way down the hill and headed straight for the grilled peaches tent.

They had some celebrities drop in as well. The director of the symphony was a regular. The mayor was a fan. Mickey would give him a free one every once in a while because he was, you know, the mayor. It wasn't the key to the city but the he said it was the key to his stomach.

The producer of wonderful films would come by and seemed generally amused by the goings on. His eyes soaked up the sea of shoppers but were paying attention to the little details. Although he would just be looking around with a smile through his bearded white face covering, it was as if he was holding up his hands to make a film frame and was looking through his hand lens. Mickey's friend had worked on projects with him for years, having his start in the art department at a recording studio. When he got laid off twenty years ago, he set up a studio with Mickey. He called it "Reality Studio" which was a play on words but also the truth of his new self-employed lifestyle. Phil went on to his own fame in the movie business, but always stopped by to see the Saul. They played a little game each time. Saul would look alarmed, call security and ask him how he got into his office. Phil enjoyed his annexed lifestyle at his "Reality Studio" but reveled in this little interaction like a kid blowing up firecrackers.

And that is how they all wound up together in Reality Studio. There was no fantasy about it. And there were no regular checks coming in either. "A man needs a place to hang his hat" they used say.

Mickey learned some of the essentials of photography here: how to stay up when you are down; how to get the money up front and never put film in the camera until the people were actually in the studio. "Always get the money up front" he was told by the old pro, "If they can't pay in advance, then they can't pay in retreat". These were rules to live by. This is why so many photographers fail out there. They know how to take the photos but don't keep the business going. Art and Business – such a lifestyle!

Home Sweet Home

Little Tommy was in the corner playing with his fire truck. If he was ever asked what he wanted to be when he grew up, the answer was immediate and delivered without hesitation, "I want to be a fireman!"

Mickey sat in the corner taking it all in. He had no children in fact he had no wife, and wasn't seeing somebody new. This was what he might have said a year ago or four. It was his modus operandi throughout his thirties, leaving him alone most of the time. "What it is" one of his Afro friends used to say. But he enjoyed being with his friends families, watching the little ones grow up.

Jack, Tommy's brother got up from playing with his own toys and Tommy, seeing him get to his feet, put down his fire truck, bolted with great speed towards Jack, hitting him low and hard. Jack hit the carpet hard after the open field tackle but laughed out loud and came right after Tommy, trying to give him some payback. With amusement, Mickey sipped on his beer, grinning at the mother who ineffectually yelled at him "Tommy, leave your brother alone."

Beth was making pizza but Coach wasn't home yet, out making a living and running his business. She had the pizza stone on the counter and the dough had been sitting there at room temperature for a few hours, covered in corn meal. This way the dough doesn't get crisp and stale on the outside. She began punching it with closed fist, making it submit to a circle shape as best she could. Then with the tips of her three fingers she evened out the depth and shored up the uneven edges to make the pie. She used half the prescribed amount of dough for a couple of reasons, the first being that it was half the carbs. Eating well and watching calories is what she did. The other reason was that thin pizza was what it was all about-forget this thick Chicago style deep dish that everyone was talking about.

Her idea of pizza was New York. She waxed nostalgic for those small little pizza shops downtown where you stood, facing the wall and ate your slice. "Tommy, go help your brother get ready for dinner honey. And put your toys away first" she said without looking away from the counter and the salad preparation. Tommy pretended like he didn't hear a word, turning away from her and playing even harder with whatever toy tickled his fancy. "Tommy" she barked a few decibels louder to get his attention. "Aw mom" came the weeping painful response.

Mickey thought of what his own response would have been and figured it would be pretty much the same. But he didn't think that he was as smart as Tommy at that age. Decisively less informed and lacking the salesmanship of these youngsters; it amazed him and made him wonder. He wondered about his own self as well as queries about his own possible offspring.

Coach's family was a surrogate for him. He watched his kids grow from day one, seeing Tommy even before him, as he was out of town working and couldn't get back. Tommy was the size of a loaf of bread then and Mickey suffered not in seeing every little growth stage. He was always there and seemed to show up right before dinner, eating with the family and being privy to the tantrums both child and adult. For a few years he was there so often that they would cook a little more, knowing he would probably show up anyway. There were the birthdays and Hanukkah and barbeques in the summer.

Coach went through an early grumpy old man stage and/or was too tired to go out and have fun with his young wife. Mickey would fill in for him going to concerts and parties as he stayed home with the kids, falling asleep on the couch. Beth was a Brooklyn girl that just wanted to have fun and every once in a while had to get a little crazy. Mickey, having never been married, didn't really understand the delicate nuisances of maintaining a long term relationship and figured he was just tagging along anyway. They would hit some clubs in San Francisco and dance till late and meet up with some friends and party. He figured that they were both doing what they wanted in this crazy life. Once Beth introduced him as her surrogate husband and although it was really a joke there was some truth to it. More like girlfriends she would confide in him things which sometimes blurred his role into a genderless canister which in the end was all about deep friendship and connectivity.

"Mom, Jack is stealing all my blocks and messing everything up from where I had it. He's always doing it" the five-year old said with an eloquence crafted out of preparation. It was always and never. Those were where the weary battle lines were drawn with the brothers. Mickey thought about one of his relationship endings or explosions and connected the two in his mind. Once things get polar, he thought, there was no coming back together again. Keeping things closer to the middle ground of compromise and cooperation was the only thing that kept things connected. That and family. With family there is the powerful umbilical cord that rings an acoustic chord of unity, regardless of where you are or how apart you become. With friends, there is only a celebration of the now, where you are on your journey and the connectivity that comes with that. Once you move on to other interests or areas of growth then that connection is either lost or another connection bond develops.

"Mickey, what happened to that Brazilian girl you dated last summer? Do you two still see each other?" Mickey shuffled a little side to side as he thought of the best way to put it. "Not really. We had the big breakup and that was about it. " Beth used some large wooden forks and was mixing together the salad with some peppers, tomatoes and red onion that she had been cutting up. "There, that is done. It looks damn good if I don't say so myself. So, I thought you guys got back together after that. But nothing huh?"

"Yeah there was that one time when we met at the bar shooting pool. We went to my cottage and did the nasty and it was hot. But it wasn't as hot as normal. There was something missing. I really liked her but when we got together again it wasn't the same. You know fucking isn't everything"

"Mickey, I can't believe you! Watch your damn language would you!"

Tommy was on this like a judge. "Mommy said damn! Mommy said a bad word. What is fucking Mommy" Beth shot Mickey a look that could cut stone. "Mickey and Mommy both said bad words. But we are sorry we were bad…both of us, aren't we Mickey." Looking at him now with that same stone-knife gaze, Mickey grumbled that he too was sorry It seemed to satisfy Tommy and he was ready for something new again. "Now go and wash your hands and get ready for dinner honey. See what your brother is doing over by the stereo and both of you get on the couch and watch TV for a while." She went over to the fridge and pulled out a chilled bottle of wine and asked him if he wanted some and he said of course yes. "So, no one in the cue Mickey, no hot leads?" Mickey stuttered no but said he had met an interesting women at the supermarket and that they had talked. "You know when you go out with a women with children it is a whole different matter. They aren't just looking at you with the standard checklist but are evaluating you as the future father figure for their children. They seem to look you over top to bottom as if they are buying a used car. You know what I mean?" Beth nodded yes, but pursued him further. She was always looking out for him, trying to set him up. She was at times his Jewish Mother, sometimes his old girlfriend, although they had never dated, and always his bubbala, the enduring word for Jewish Godmother.

It went on like this over at their house all the time. It was so different from his own house which was quiet until he turned on the television. It's not like he was there every day really, but he showed up a lot. He'd get his fill of 'family-land' usually leaving when the kid started getting cranky and wouldn't take a bath. Bath time was usually his signal to leave. Eight-thirty still seemed early to him, but he wasn't on the get up early train anyway. He was a bit of a night owl, and didn't get up before seven-thirty ever.

Beth had the pizza dough spread out now. Her secret was to work it awhile and then leave it be, going back to it in ten minutes or so. It gave the dough a chance to loosen up. Once it was almost two inches from the edge she would get out the roller and with a furious concentration, spread it evenly beyond the edge of the pizza stone, letting it hang over the side. Satisfied, she would put the roller down and gently fold the dough inside the edge about one inch, packing it down to make a proper crust.

"I though you put the sauce down first, then the cheese" Beth smiled when she heard the question and jibbed him that he didn't really know anything about cooking anyway. She laughed a cackle as she reached for glass of Chardonnay and smiled as she sipped. "No, no you are right, that's the way it is normally done" and she continued with the spreading of cheese which was done in quick time. Once there was an even amount she grabbed the bowl of pesto that she had made earlier simply from the basil in the back yard, some olive oil and garlic. She splashed it around in purposefully random designs and it looked an Irish green on top of the white mozzarella. "Coach and I went out to that restaurant, you know that new place up on Broadway". Mickey caught a runaway child named Tommy who was not listening to his mother and doing laps around the kitchen island. "Broadway in San Francisco?" Tommy struggled from his grasp. Jack yelled from the other room, the telephone rang. "No, no in Oakland. On Broadway up by the car dealerships. I know this is a marketing call. I'm not going to pick it up. Doesn't that piss you off Mickey."

The message started in and she picked up immediately recognizing the slowness of her husband's speech. There were a lot of "ahaa, ahaa, ok." She hung up with a "be careful honey, we'll see you soon".

"He's stuck in the City but he's on his way." Mickey knew that he wouldn't be home before bath time and that he would see him tomorrow.

"Ok, so you went to a new restaurant and......."

"Oh yeah, so we went to Zees and we ordered a little pizza appetizer that came out on a pizza tray about twelve inches wide and we loved it. They made it just this way, putting the cheese down first, then the sauce, but not so much of it and then the toppings. I'm doing my own thing tonight with the toppings, but it is the same approach. They used asparagus as the only topping. It works really well on a thin crust because it doesn't absorb the sauce so much." She continued to work the pizza and within two minutes it was ready for the oven. Tonight's was simple. She had prepared an entire head of garlic into little pieces. Using the side of a large block knife place on top of the cloves, she would slam her fist hard and when revealed all it needed was to have the skin peel off. The pile was pulled together and the cleaver rapidly minced the pieces. She had chicken breasts cut into little strips that had already been partially cooked. "Pizza is great Mickey, you can use whatever is left in the fridge, just throw it on top. This chicken is from last night. Sometimes I use vegetables that are about to go bad or even leftovers. You can do Mexican pizza or left over spaghetti pizza. The kid's love it, you know, Tommy and his Dad."

"You do have three boys don't you." Beth smiled loudly. She wasn't the kind of person that looked happy all the time, not that there was a grimace there really. But when she smiled it was like a rainbow after a week of rain.

"So did he talk with you about the ski trip?" Mickey didn't understand the question exactly as it wasn't really the time of the year when they were planning the annual escape. "No, what do you mean?"

"I want to go skiing with you guys this year in Wyoming or Utah, or wherever it is you are going." Mickey understood a number of things at the same moment. It was clear from her tone that she wanted to go and was pressuring Coach to be included. Also, he knew immediately that Coach had done some sidestepping around the issue. He was the type that would go four blocks out of his way to avoid a confrontation. He would slide it down to the next time they met sometimes but most likely he was in avoidance mode. He acted like there was nothing to discuss, copasetic to a degree. He just didn't go there. So it was obvious to Mickey, knowing them both well, that Beth was pressuring him to bring it up and that he had not.

"Well, no, what are you talking about?" He looked steady into the eyes of Beth trying to gage the intensity. She held his gaze longer than expected which signaled high intensity.

"Unbelievable. He said he was going to talk with you about this last week. You guys didn't talk about the ski trip? She was at the cutting board, cutting up some vegetables that she was going to steam for Jack when she turned towards him emphasizing her words with the knife she was holding in her right hand. As she made her point she got closer to him she motioned with the large butcher block knife to make her point. "I went on the other trip and I know it's been awhile but I really miss going and would like to ski. You guys have developed this thing as a Boys Club kind of thing and I just think it's stupid. We can only get out of town so often with the kids and everything and it's all about the January ski trip this, and no women allowed and what kind of crap is that anyway?" Emphatically motioning with the knife she made her final point with the tip of the knife almost resting on Mickey's chest. He had risen to his toes and arched his back up over the counter and up against the cabinet in a playful way to let her know how close she was getting with the knife. "Ah, ah, ah, I wasn't there, I didn't do it" This made her laugh. as she had not realized how close she had come to him with a sharp knife.

She turned back to her work at the cutting board but it was clear how passionate she felt about it. "I don't know Beth, there is a fairly established ethos here, but I'm not exactly the decider, I don't make decisions for everyone, I'm not a dictator."

"Yeah, but they do look to you to organize the damn thing." Mickey laughed out loud at that because he never considered himself a ringleader. "You know it's Dutch more than anyone. He the one with the issues about getting away from everything. He believes in some kind of male utopian experience or something. I'm just looking to ski Beth. Skiing without issues, that my agenda. So, you should have Coach bring it up with Dutch."

"Yeah, like that's going to happen. I mean we all got busy with our jobs and raising families so you tell me, what is it going to take?"

"I don't know, during that time we developed some kind of male culture on the trips. We walk around in underwear, fart, play poker all the time and ski. I know the women think we are up there getting into some kind of trouble but it really quite simple pleasures. It's all about skiing."

"I'm all about skiing too Mickey." He didn't really think so, but didn't want to bring it up. In the back of his mind all he could remember was her not skiing but going shopping or taking a sleigh out to watch the feeding of the elk herd. She made Coach do girly tourist things that distracted him from skiing. "I know you are" he lied. "But it's really about the boys getting together and celebrating the fact that we can get away and have fun.

"Well, maybe I'll just start a women's ski trip then." She was getting a terse tone in her voice which didn't bode well. He thought this was something she felt strongly about and she wasn't going to let go. Beyond that, he was thinking that maybe Coach was right about dodging the issues and not talking about it.

"Okay, let's talk about it then." He said, opting for a different track. "What is your deal, what do you think is going on with this. It's not like we don't want you to come because you don't fit in or something. It's simply a gender issue. It's nothing personal, it's just that you are…..you know….a woman!"

"Oh that is just BULLSHIT you know that Mickey." She said the word with vigor but quietly, assuring that no children would hear it. "Ok, Okay, I'm not sure it is but I respect where you're coming from. Of all the women I know, you're the only one I would vote for. You know you are one of my favorite people, forget male or female and we've skied before together, but there are others with stronger feelings about it. Maybe some of the married guys like getting away from their wives. You know I don't know anything about that, so don't shoot the messenger."

The pizza was in the oven and Beth went over to look in the glass and see how it was doing. Keeping it at over five hundred degrees was the secret she told him as he came over for a look see. "So, you don't think that men and women can ski together and live in a ski house?"

"No, no that's not what I'm saying at all. It's just that that would be a different kind of a trip. Maybe we should do a couples ski week up in Tahoe or something. What else is bugging you about it"

"I don't know. I really don't know what's got me all riled up. Maybe it's that I was on that other trip and that seemed to work with you and Bobby didn't it?"

"Yeah, but that was a long time ago sister. I guess it doesn't really matter, but the last trip we had there were a total of nine guys on the trip, and I don't know where they are at with this, probably just sitting on the sidelines like your husband is eh?" That bristled her a little bit. "Come on. He didn't bring it up did he, you did." If you want him as your main advocate here, you need to work that out with him, you know. I don't want to get in the middle of a married couple, especially when both of them are friends of mine. I knew you before he even met you but I've known him for a long time. It kind of puts me in a difficult situation." The oven timer bell went off and she got her oven mitts on and removed the stone, putting it on the counter on top of a wood cutting board. "The secret is letting it just sit on the stone for a while. It cooks the underneath and keeps the pizza warm as well. I put this lid on top of it and leave it about ten minutes before I slice it up. It tends to crystallize the sugars in the sauce and pulls it all together."

"I would have to say I'm conflicted now. I'm leaning towards two separate trips maybe but when the guys get together or we are out there in the Wasatch, the mood changes about just keeping it simple, and women are, and I tell you this in confidence that..." Beth started laughing and slapped back "Ah come on you've just got to be kidding with man-trip thing, come on, give me a break."

"Yes being in the man-cave has its moments you know, there is simplicity with the poker and camaraderie of the day and then there's football you know, it's kind of a man thing too, no?" Beth was getting the kids dinner together, noodles and hot dogs. They didn't like the fancy pizzas and Beth didn't even try, so she just gave them what they wanted. Tommy was fed in a normal way but Jack had to be plugged into a high chair which only lit him up. There were the cliché and predictable tantrum about mostly about the other's food and there was the obligatory food tossing commanding a terse retort from Mom. She had taken the top of the pizza stone and using a super large spatula, she made sure there were no sticky spots that would make it stick, Picking up two matching oven mitts, she slid the pizza off the stone and onto a cutting board. She slowly ran the round pizza cutter up slowly and then down slowly, 12 to 6 o'clock and back and forth. Then, harder she went back and forth again. Turning the pizza she did it three more times, plucking off a piece of chicken as she admired her work. Then, she slid the whole thing onto a circular metal tray, like the ones you get in a pizza parlor. There it was, done.

They had both been thinking about what was said. Mickey opened "with all that, consider this; it has been suggested by some, I'm not saying who- in fact I will deny flatly that I ever said this, that there are some that believe in a certain sanctity of Boy's Club. We are out there in the wild and the testosterone is flying and we are like an Indian tribe or something.

So, no squaws, is what I've heard. I know that's pissing you off."

"Ya think?" She was fine towards the end of her second glass of chardonnay. He hugged her hard when they parted. The next hour or so was busy with the boys. The slightest irregularity, like a missing toy, might make things ugly ending an otherwise serene evening. Mickey thought he would retreat to his quiet little cottage and left towards home at the cottage.

The Waiting

"Ok" Mickey sighed. "We will just get together and talk it out". There was silence, prolonged, neither wanting to really say how strongly they felt or address the issues. And there were issues. Right now it was the elephant in the living room kind of issue, but that would soon change. Beth wanted to come on the ski trip. Mickey really wanted things to stay the same as did most everyone, except Coach who was bowing to the wants of Beth. It wasn't an unreasonable request, after all, and one that could be implemented. Mickey's idea was to have a meeting where all would just put it on the table and get it out in the open. He called all the guys and everyone said they would be there about eight. He told them it was "eight skate and donate". He had learned that laying down the request for money early was a key factor in the successful acquisition of ski funds for the cabin.

The plan was set for a meeting at the studio after Coach's Creek game. In the studio Mickey had a headshot session for a hip hop artist through an agent type guy that he had worked with in the last year. Just thinking about it for a second started to piss him off but then, there it was, kind of funny too.

He had shot Dre once for the same people who said they had a mansion all set up for a photo shoot for an album cover. Working with hip hop entertainers was always fun because of their creativity- it excited his photographic palate. He followed them threw the stone guardhouse at the gated community. The two new BMW's were lined up at the gatehouse where the guard waved them through. Mickey followed in his twenty-five year old Plymouth. Arriving at a lavish Mediterranean Estate he was asked to work quickly. They shot around the pool and patio scene. Turned out that nothing was reserved for the shoot and the manager, slick like, just said they wanted to buy the place and look around.

That was in the white suburbs but this time he was up on the Crest, where it was like the wild west- life was cheap and it was all about who you ran with.

"Just don't leave me up here" Mickey said with that side look of his and he thought for a second that they understood each other. A few minutes later he forgot about that notion. In that moment he reflected upon himself like one of those detectives in an old Perry Mason episode "Chinatown, another gum shoe photographer working on the frontiers of photography"

"Oh man, you know I'm in, man". Mickey instantly thought this the kind of dualistic language that meant, or could mean a number of things, depending on the need.

"Just don't leave me up there………" and the music agent was off; punching it hard right up the steep California hills and Mickey's jaw dropped. Mr. Music guy/manager slash you can only get the guy in voicemail and sometimes he would drop off the planet for days at a time, was up the hill and gone. Firing up the Root Beer Brown 1975 Plymouth Custom was a relief as it was not something to be taken for granted.

The car was named Eldon. Mickey had bought it on eBay from a guy whose father, Eldon, passed and he had to sell the beast. So, naturally the car became Eldon. Fifty Six Thousand miles and well cared for it was steady and efficient transportation. But they were going through some times. Mickey and Eldon had a rocky relationship but they stayed together and rode it out. Mickey would throw money into Eldon when there was no choice, swearing "this is the last time. No really!"

So it was taken as a good sign when Eldon fired up and pursued the low paying job up the hill. It was a neighborhood of homes built in the sixties, poorly and on small lots. He was sure they called it the hood, or some other words that really meant ghetto but outward appearances said otherwise. They were gentle serene homes, except for the outright neglect.

Most of them looked like a fresh coat of paint and a little landscaping would make them normal and almost appealing

The guy was going to give him some money when they met, but of course they never got out of their cars. There were a few rules of the trade and getting paid up front was high on the list. When you're living project to project, then following the money is key.

Mickey was following the money up the top of the Crest. He had never heard of it and it was increasingly becoming obvious why. It started with a couple of shuttered homes, then homes that had been burned and then boarded up. There were bars on the windows and there were bars on the doors. The higher they went up the worse it got. There were a lot of people on the corners now and they eye-followed Mickey, gauging his every move as he stayed ever so close to the agents car careening up the suburban streets

Mickey was raised to see everyone the same. There was no Puerto Rican, no African no other's, only the equality that his Mother had taught him and the peace it brought. But this isn't how the world saw things and thinking this way had him in trouble on more than one occasion. Mostly he would be in a place that he didn't belong and was out of his element.

Being in The Crest was decisively out of his element. The brothers were out in numbers and they were eying whitey knowing more than him that he didn't belong there. The looks were not looks of hatred or of racism but more of disbelief. What was he doing here? Crossing one large intersection and heading still up the hill, they passed what must have been at least fifty or so Young Black Brothers mulling around the corner with dark baggy jackets and a shiftless, restless energy that only holds hands with drug dealers and the dark side. Cruising by about twenty miles an hour, Mickey had the window down and his arm hanging casually over the side of the door, as if to say he was unarmed, was not a cop and didn't really care what they were up to.

Mickey was following the agent's bumper with a tenth of an inch distance at this point. There was no mistaking the two cars were together. They rounded a corner slowing to about fifteen miles per hour. Eldon glided with elegance as root beer shades caught their interest now as much as the white boy. Eldon did sparkle and although it was just a stupid looking Plymouth and not a car of choice with this generation, the paint looked cool on anything. Another ten blocks up the hill and Mickey was relieved as the agent pulled up to the curb and came to an abrupt stop in front of an abandoned shuttered home.

"See, what did I tell you" the agent smiled.

"You didn't tell me anything man. We didn't really talk until we met at the Denny's at the bottom of the hill and then you took off like a bat. Why did you do that?"

Agent man had pulled up out front of a typical suburban home except that it was boarded up. There was garbage piled high in the front yard with a bunch of tires on top of a big pile of things that you couldn't instantly tell what it was or what it was apart of .

"You got my money man?" Agent man let out a sigh but also let out with a pile of cash. Mickey had done a couple of little jobs for him and he always got his cash. And they always paid cash, these hip hop guys. No one ever cares where the cash comes from but it would often make Mickey wonder when he received it. As he handed the cash over, the agent started talking about the shots and how it was really going to be all that. Although there was no one at the property when they pulled up, Mickey looked up from his camera bag and saw about six guys that had appeared quietly. Names were flying around that he had never heard of before, surnames all…. Jayzee, Swopman, DC, and Bab.

"What do you think of this as a background" agent man said, as they pulled around the back of the house and Mickey started to set up.

"I don't know………I supposed it could work" Mickey said stalling, looking around the whole time for something else that would work better. "So you're going for a burned out building look, huh?"

"Man it's cool , we're just going to get everyone in front of the deck here and make it happen You tell us what you want, but when they get here, it will just come together." Mickey sighed a bit and wasn't thinking Grammy at this point in his life anyway and started to just think about getting out of there.

Mickey set up the shot and took a Polaroid so he could see the lighting. The first guy there agreed to be a test shot and he just stood in front of the camera like a stone, but it was enough to get an idea.". Just before he snapped the Polaroid, Jayzee ran over to the bushes by the fence and pulled out a weapon. It looked like an automatic machine gun, but Mickey didn't really know guns and disliked them all equally. Jayzee held the gun with the meanest look he could muster for an eighteen year old and held that weapon like an African hunter on safari or those old sepia photos from the Wild West in the 1800's.

"How many did you say were going to be in the shot?" Mickey was thinking how wide the shot would be and how the background would extend beyond the subject.

Polaroid's took about sixty seconds to develop and Mickey used that time to look around. Looking up from the relative security of his camera bag, he noticed that there were now about fifteen soldiers in the back yard now, and they all had guns: handguns, shotguns, serious looking automatic rifles and the like. And they were holding them at all different angles, up in the air, sideways, anywhere but down.

The agent liked the Polaroid, said it looked like it was "all that". One of the lanky gun wielding gangsters came over and said "Yeah, man, its dank". The agent took a closer look and agreed, "Dank", he said.

Mickey had to object "Man what are you guys talking about- it looks well lighted on all sides and the background comes up lit too. Seems light balanced to me."

They all had a little laugh and went back to the porch where they were practicing their looks and gun holding. "No man it's good" the Agent managed, looking at it again with a big smile on his face, shaking his head slightly

"So what are you saying, man" Mickey started, for a minute defending his lighting. He was pointing to the background and the contrast. He had tried to balance the light from his light to the background and keep detail in the shade areas of the porch. The manager was grinning widely now and Mickey got the idea that he was entertaining this guy, making his day "No dank, dude. It's a dank. It's a good thing."

"Yeah man that is dank. Digity Dank" said a guy right over Mickey's shoulder that he had not noticed before. It startled him and it was unexpected.

That was a good thing, dank, Mickey thought. He wondered how he missed that though, he tried to stay up on the latest. He found out later that "dank" had been around for a while. Within a week, he was hearing it everywhere. He heard it on the David

Letterman Show. It was just another reminder that he was getting old.

Turning around now, he was confronted by the cold reality that there were twenty or so heavily armed criminals that were now looking at him. The Agent nervously brushed by him and muttered "maybe we should get this thing going." Mickey was stuck in neutral for a minute. His motor was running by not much else was on. Like one of those bad dreams where you want to run but your feet are stuck in the ground. Mickey snapped like]a snap pea, started moving people around, just telling them to stand here or knell down in front. None were too excited about kneeling down in front, thinking it was not the alpha position. Mickey broke into his baseball announcer voice about "being in the front row" and finally got a few of them in that position. The immediate challenge which had to be solved in the next sixty seconds or so was that they were all standing the same way. Mickey gave up and started posing them like one of those old west shots of the posse standing over the captured Indian's body or the like.

He got off one photo and looked through the lens and saw one of the guys pointing his automatic weapon right at him. He now wanted to get this thing over with. When the subject starts pointing loaded weapons at the camera it was time to leave. But just then, when he was taking the second shot, the sirens started; maybe two sirens together, whirling up the hill and in their direction.

What happened next was visceral. Someone yelled "It the nabbers man. Hit the fence". And hit the fence they did. With athletic grace they put guns in pockets and jumped the fence like they did it every day or so. It was business as usual. Within fifteen seconds the back yard was empty and Mickey was standing there alone with his camera in hand and was switching his gaze from his light to his gear bag to the fence, and back again. He thought the Agent went out front to check on things but he soon realized that he had disappeared too. Looking around again he realized he was alone in the Crest.

As quickly as he could but with his regular routine, he broke down, taking apart his camera first and then his lights. Umbrellas down and stands recessed, he was now ready to leave this backyard studio complete with ghetto staging. He went around the side of the house he walked down. He could see immediately that the Agents Beamer was gone. There were some curious neighbors out on their driveways just doing the normal looking around stuff when they hear sirens in the distances.

Mickey started loading gear into the trunk and was thinking about how great it would be to have an assistant right now. Two would be nice. Just then a loudly colored blue sedan pulled up alongside and Mickey moved in seemingly slow motion as his head looked up and to the side. He was almost relieved to see a car full of wide eyed children and their mom. She was about three hundred pounds and was very round, wearing a flower print dress. She kept the car running as she leaned across the front seat, saying "They told me there was a white boy up here getting into trouble and I just couldn't believe it. Are you crazy or something? What do you think you are doin' up here anyway? Are you crazy or something?"

As Mickey was trying to come up with a good answer, at least one that made sense, he began to wonder, indeed, what was he doing up here?

Just then, the police vehicle crawled up slowly and stopped right in the middle of the street and the officer got out slowly, looking around the street and talking on his shoulder-strap walkie-talkie. There were crackling sounds and codes being issued, but he couldn't quite make out what was being said. The officer came directly to the trunk of Eldon where the photographer was closing up his last gear bag. He looked inquisitively; eyes wide open and his hand near enough his gun to make it obvious.

"Is everything alright sir? Do you feel alright? Said the Crest's finest.

"Well yeah, I'm okay. What can I do for you?" Mickey said looking the officer directly in the eyes.

"There have been a lot of reports coming through about activity up here and some kind of trouble with a white boy and guns"

"Hey all I know is that I was taking some photos for an album cover and then everyone started running away, I packed up my gear and here I am. I was working for a manager but I haven't seen him either". Mickey thought that should just about cover it. The officer starred at him for a few seconds and then plainly said "Well, you have a good day sir", walked back to his squad car and headed down the hill.

Mickey didn't stay around too much longer than that and noticed that he was the center of attention to all the neighbors who were still outside their homes and whose attention was spiked by the appearance of law enforcement.

Eldon once again fired up like the dependable transportation that it wasn't and Mickey slowly drove away. In a heartbeat he realized he didn't really know how to get out of here. He had been following the Agent up the hill and was so consumed with looking around at the goings on he hadn't paid attention to street signs. Pulling forward he knew one thing. He had to go down the hill. Down and out to the freeway. Like a lost hiker following a stream, he would just keep going downstream.

Winding down into a broad opened intersection, Mickey saw the craps game as he came around the corner and the whole group of thirty to forty came into focus. He knew it was a crap game because he had seen them down by the studio. It was all done very quickly with loud cackle and cheers. The guys who lose don't cackle too much, but everyone yells when the dice are rolled. Money flies around on the ground as the pass line bets are made. The dice crashed up against the cardboard box and land like heroes getting a hero's welcome.

It was Street Craps, not to be confused with anything that might happen in a casino or an organized game. For one thing, there was no house. One of the young mavericks, feeling lucky or particularly fat, money wise, would be the house. It was the fastest way to make money, as the house always has the advantage. But you had to have a bankroll, as there can always be those times when the house takes a hit. In the long run the house will come out. Over an eight hour period, the house would always be on top, but here on the street the games might be short lived and everyone could win. The dealer better have the scratch or there would be hell to pay.

The game came to a slight stop as everyone looked up to see Mickey sliding by with his arm out the window, both hands easily seen with his right hand on the top part of the steering wheel and his eyes straight forward, not taking the chance of a casual eye contact that could be misconstrued as a form of alpha behavior. Sometimes it could only take the slightest look and a guy goes off. They were all leaning forward or bent on their knees playing this wild street version of craps, but as Mickey drove by there was a simultaneous straightening up and turning of the heads. With equal ballet graciousness they bent back over, knelt back down and got back to the serious business of making some easy money.

In his rear view mirror Mickey could make out the shapes leaning over and peering into the game. He was glad that was behind him. He felt like he was headed in the right direction, was glad he had the money in his pocket and although he only had one photo and a test Polaroid, his day was going to get back to normal now.

For a second he saw what he thought was the freeway. Then it disappeared. He seemed to be going on the back side of the hill now and his heart was beating a little faster as he saw an older Black man with a straw hat and overalls working in his garden. Mickey thought for a second about asking for directions but decided to plunge ahead.

Just at that moment a car full of four men lurched out into his lane about two feet. The car was parked and was pulling out as the driver had neglected to look for oncoming vehicles and thought he would just look as he entered the lane. Mickey instinctually slammed on the brakes and Eldon screeched to a stop within an inch of a nicely polished Lexus with white leather interior. He thought about doing the wave, as if to say, Hey – my fault – have a nice day" then he thought better of it. "Don't make eye contact and keep moving," he reminded himself.

Mickey moved slowly forward and thought for a minute that he had dodged a bullet. He heard a loud burning of tires sound and looking in his rear view mirror he could see the Lexus had screeched out of its parking spot and was in fast pursuit of him. He was about a block ahead of them and came to a stop at the stop sign. The Lexus was without doubt after him, it was now clear. Mickey stayed stopped at the light and watched as the Lexus went from zero to sixty in a few seconds and then slid to a stop to his left, tires burning to a stop. The Lexus had abruptly come to a stop next to him at the stop sign, but on the other side of the street in the oncoming lane. Mickey looked over to his left, knowing that he could not avoid them this time. He probably should have acknowledged their near collision and figured they were pissed about that.

There were no words said. Not a soul around to be seen. As Mickey looked over to the other car that had their windows down now, he saw all four men with their right hands crossed over their chests apparently reaching for their weapons. They were poised for retaliation now and were gazing at him for what seems like an eternity. He couldn't see any weapons but didn't want to assume for a second that they weren't there.

Mickey thought of something to say for a second and then just did what came naturally to him. He smiled, and slowly raised his left hand, keeping his right hand on the top of the steering wheel in plain sight, and shot them a peace sign. A big beautiful peace sign and then he said "Hey man! Sorry about that"

The four brothers just looked at him in disbelief. The one in the front passenger seat, clearly letting his gun drop back in his pocket, could be heard saying " Ah man, it's just a Barney" The automatic window rolled up and the Lexus peeled out, screeching, and was gone in a second, turning at the next stop sign to the right.

Mickey felt instantly that he was glad he was a Barney and that if he had been an eighteen year old Black man, he would have been shot. But he was just a Barney. Was that Barney Rubble from the Flintstones? He wasn't sure.

Five minutes later he was on the freeway and back to the studio He wondered if he would ever return to the Crest. But he loved to photograph the Hip Hop artists. They were so expressive. Unlike the staid corporate shots or even other recording artists, they had a lot of attitude and knew how to exude it.

And this is the guy he was waiting for now. Always late and predictably not on time, Mickey was fine with this though and could plan around it. The appointment was at 6pm so Mickey could often be found at Peet's, nursing a latte' at this exact moment. Knowing his client was predictably late allowed him the flexibility of being late himself to the studio, and as he was always running late and behind himself, so it all worked out.

Mickey enjoyed photographing the rappers and hip-hoppers. They always came with their game and had lots of energy, often expressing themselves with their hands and fingers for the photos, surrounded by bling and chains to highlight it.

Once Mickey was photographing one young man that was trying to make his career move in music and he kept doing the hand thing, making these simple gestures that didn't really mean anything, but said it all. Enough with all this Mickey thought "calm your soul and just give me one symbol and just take a deep breath. You are over-doing it – just be calm and look into the camera with an uncomplicated sincere look". The Hipster looked at Mickey for what seemed like forever then turned away so his back was towards the photographer. When he turned around his face was relaxed and shinned with an inner strength Mickey had not yet seen. He snapped the shot and this is one they used on the CD cover.

The Rappers were kind of funny in some ways. Mickey would ask them to bring in a change of clothes – mostly tops as most of the shots were waist up. They would show up to the studio with the jeans they were wearing, their favorite T-shirt. They would open up a suitcase and there they were – seven pairs of sneakers, tennis shoes, basketball shoes and miscellaneous athletic footwear. It was all about the footwear.

Ladies would sometimes come in with a pile of new clothes in Macy's bags. They had in fact just come from the Macy's and would wear these garments for the shoot and then return them afterwards, putting the charges on the card for just a day.

The artists and manager blew into the studio quickly. Agent Man dealt with the money quickly which Mickey appreciated and then announced that he was leaving. "You know what to do, you know what I want. Just do your thing and give me a call when I can pick them up"

He had introduced the rapper to Mickey as an initial like CDee, but at one point Mickey heard one of the rappers sidekicks call him something that sounded like it had an "r" in it, like CDree. He wasn't sure and just started calling him "C" and that seemed to work so he forgot about it..

After one test shot, which Mickey looked at for a longer time than most, he said" C, how about coming in here for some make-up for a while". C's buddies looked at him with one of those guy looks of disbelief. "Man, I ain't doin' no makeup man", Mickey sighed and was thinking of telling him why he needed make-up and then told himself "fuck it".

Half hour later, C and his boys were out of there and Mickey was waiting once again, this time for the Boys Club and ski buddies. Coach and his wife, who by all reports from the Creek game was foaming at the mouth, were on the way. Steffan was the first to call in and he was the one with the report on Coach's wife. He had work to do and couldn't make it. He was very sorry but would go along with whatever we came up with. Also, he wanted to know to where to send the cabin deposit.

The Boys called in next with a lame excuse about errant plumbing situation that needed their attention at all costs. They were very sorry and wanted to be there to discuss the trip but just couldn't get there. They were all four, as usual, complicit and in concert

Mickey began to see the writing on the wall. Just then Bobby came in. He didn't play baseball but skied with the grace of a champion. He skied with his Dad when he was five years old and loved it in a way that few could appreciate. It was a romantic poetic pursuit for Bobby that took him back in time. "No one's here yet" he asked.

"Not yet" he answered without making eye contact. A few minutes went by, Mickey putting away some lights and stands trying to think about the impending confrontation with Coach's wife. He started making small talk with Bobby but this just made him suspicious. "Were they coming right after the game? " He inquired, but Mickey could feel that he thought something was up. Bobby was unaware of last week's controversial conversation at Murphy's.

A loud pounding erupted on the door. It was Dutch. He may have used the doorbell but it would have been hard to hear above the roar of the rapping. Dutch always arrived in this manner, with a loudness that matched his personality. He hammered on the door front one more time before Mickey came to the relief of the door itself which might have splintered from yet another human hammer pounding.

Whenever Dutch entered a room it always became instantly smaller. There was the physics of it; his largeness displaced the existing space and was mathematically smaller by the shear ratio of numbers. He was a large man that seemed to take up more space than most people his size. With an amble and sway he moved thru the door jam, filling its rectangular space with his own. In the old west they would not so lovingly refer to a man like Dutch as a Jarhead. Perhaps not to his face, but that is the way with most ethnic slurs, and calling someone a Jarhead was most definitely that.

How appropriate this one seemed to fit. His large head featured fearsome eyes that usually came with a fierce unrelenting gaze that usually didn't waver. He had the eye contact of a lawyer in a murder trial or a badger eyeing his prey. This gaze came out of immensely deep eye sockets which was common with the Jarheads. His bone structure was solid with high cheek bones. His girlfriend was also a Jarhead, but she didn't have the unwavering gaze of Dutch. On the contrary she had a problem with eye contact, often looking away when engaged in conversation, eyes darting anywhere except the source. With her, there was an uneasiness that came with direct eye contact, even if the conversation was on the light side or simply passing the time. Mickey once tried to test his theories about her, and he discovered that about five seconds was her maximum eye contact time. She would look down, look around or look out the window. Sometimes when Mickey talked to her, he would look away himself so as to not make her feel nervous or threatened by the eye contact and like a good host, not wanting to make his guest feel uncomfortable he would be the first one to look away.

Mickey wondered if this was a reaction to Dutch's extreme eye contact, as if she had lost her confidence or was retreating from the challenge. A few weeks ago he had decided to engage Dutch in this eye contact duel. At Murphy's after a game, he wondered what would happen if he engaged Dutch and refused to be the first to look away. He wondered if it was indeed a game with him or wither it was just his nature. That night they were talking most likely about the game and Mickey's eye never left the cold stare of the Dutchman. Not even when Mickey leaned forward to expertly snare his beer, nor when he drew that long cool gulp, did he let his glare off the eyes of Dutch who just sitting there with his arms folded. He had a cola in front of him but he hated cola and hardly touched the drink. Mickey was listening now as others began talking or someone said something and then decided to let down his gaze. He flinched first and he had lost this game of flinch. Dutch was the master. His cell phone went off and then he blinked and the standoff was complete.

As he was talking on the phone and everyone was talking or watching the Giants game, he couldn't help but check our Dutch. He seemed to take up about one and one-half seat spots at the table as he spread out and relaxed. He leaned back in the chair and was huge in stature even in this position. He seems soiled if not downright dirty. It wasn't just the dirt from the game, a red clay look that was on many and worn like a badge of pride, not to be dusted off too much. No, this was the grime of chain saws. Dutch worked on trees and did so in the old school manner that didn't include hydraulic lift baskets and cranes. Dutch would strap on a leather harness from which he would hang a few tools including a chainsaw and his safety rope. He would step into his boot spikes one foot at a time and then strap them in two places; one at the bottom and one at the top of his knee high leather boots. The spikes were about six inches long and ran down straight from the heel area. Dutch would grab a short rope and walk it around the diameter of the three foot wide tree. With a grunt he would take that first step, planting the spike into the side of the bark and starting with baby steps as he got started up the tree. Once he got into his zone, he would make fairly good speed and be up at one of the top branches in a just a few seconds. Once up top, he would tie off his belie rope and would lower his position to the work area, suspending totally from the above branch. The Chainsaw would be humming in idle and Dutch would bring it up the four feet to his hands and start working.

And this is what Mickey was thinking of as they waited for everyone to show up .He knew that Dutch wasn't going to contribute much, just look at everyone "Where were they" he checked his cell phone and wondered.

A moment later the doorbell rang and Mickey made his way to the door. Coach came in first, only shooting a look at Mickey as if he was expecting incoming mortar attacks. Beth slammed the Jeep door hard turning towards the studio door and blew past Mickey like a summer storm in the Rockies. He shut the door quietly and turned to face the music

She had that look in her eye and Mickey knew this was not going to work out very well. He had been anticipating a defiant Beth all day. It was the second look that he picked up from Coach that threw him off. He hadn't expected any wavering from the Coach who was always the steady one, linear and always pointed towards the finish line. He sensed some level of exasperation from the Coach, which he wasn't ready for. He couldn't pull it together right now, right in the heat of battle but later that night he figured out that it wasn't him, it was her. The coach must have had a go with Beth. It was clear to him later after things calmed down.

But right at this moment he was being hit by both sides. Mickey was, at one point, looking back and forth between the two like he was watching a tennis match. In the middle of one of these back and forth, he caught Bobby's eye if for only one moment and it seemed that Bobby was restless. He didn't like any kind of arguments or confrontation. He would walk a mile to avoid it and he knew he just wasn't very good at confronting. In the middle of this drawn out two second glance, Mickey got the slightest feeling that

Bobby was looking for the door and might not be there the next time he glanced his way.

"Unbelievable" Beth was in his face now. He wasn't really even hearing the words anymore. They bounced off him sounded like the teachers in the Charlie Brown TV special programs….Wasaaaaaa…Woooooo….Wassssaaaaaa. For a moment he didn't even try to listen and remembered just looking at her lips move up and down with a cadence he had never noticed before.

"How embarrassing…I keep score for all the fucking games and besides I was on that other ski trip and that wasn't so bad was it. For Christ sake what is your fucking problem. Who the hell do think you are anyway some kind of great skier " Before she was done she had touched on a couple of sensitive areas to get into Mickey's head, like what he did or didn't do on the first trip, women's liberation, his failed marriage and possibly calling into question his business acumen.

"Well….. I a…we didn't…..I……You know I…….." Mickey was officially confused now. Where were the assembled masses from that night in the pub who would confront Beth with the assembled message that no women were allowed on the ski trip. The strength in numbers was not there. Coach was obviously trying to please his wife and keep peace in the henhouse. Bobby was in disengaging mode. There was no point in continuing, but this was his turf and he had to try.

"There's nothing wrong with a little separation from the species. The Indians did it. They made the women go to different sweat tents when they had their periods. Ok, maybe that wasn't a very good example", gesturing furtively towards his boys and not getting anything there he looked back at Beth and she was screaming mad. She was uttering these little remarks under her breath and she was walking around the studio looking at some of the sets and then he could hear "fucking bullshit". Then it would quiet for a bit and heard something that sounded like "asshole". Mickey was having trouble with understanding her rage, but he could understand how he would feel if the girls had left him out of a ski trip. And then he remembered that the women did a girls ski trip a few years ago and he was thinking of a non-hostile way of bringing that up. To Beth it probably seemed like he was simply spacing out and avoiding her.

And then it was silent expect for the radio which Mickey hadn't even realized was on. One look at the quiet Bobby told him that the boy had been victimized. He was looking at the floor, taking a drag on that Camel cigarette and not really looking up. It was as though he had just been through something….had survived a conflict or conquered a summit. Whatever it was, it was over and Bobby wouldn't be the same for some time, brooding over what was said. He would lift his head and stare off into the studio and seem to concentrate for a long time on something out there – a stand or a roll of paper. His concentration on a small little area was a meditation for him. It helped him cope with what he was not accustomed. "The conflict has ended" Mickey told him. Bobby said "I'm going to Murphy's. Are you coming?"

"Give me a minute". Half hour later and they were gone to the pub. He didn't expect to find any of the ski trip party there and was surprised to see the Construction House Boys, sitting at a table watching a baseball game with many empty pints in front of them. "How did that plumbing job go guys" he said as he headed to the bar. They all kind of grumbled "Yeah, great. Got er done."

"Yeah, right" they could hear Coach say as he came in the other door and went right to their table. They talked for a few minutes as Mickey stood over at the bar, about thirty feet away. He was now ordering two beers. It took a while as Murphy was laboriously constructing three Irish Coffees for some folks at the other end. It was the house specialty and had to be made just right. Only real cream was allowed and the whiskey was always Jameson's. Instead of putting a dollop on top emptied from a can like most bartenders did it, at Murphy's it was topped with a layer of real sweetened cream that really brought out the flavor. Mickey wasn't minding the wait, as it was giving him some badly needed time to think about things and what to say to Coach. He was looking to his left down the bar to the table in the corner. Coach didn't sit down. He was standing there like he was waiting for a train.

Beers in hand, Mickey headed over to the table and it was Coach who spoke first, extending his right arm to pluck the creamy pint. "We have to talk", he said, and swung around to the door. Lighting up a smoke, Coach said nothing. Mickey was thinking about how mad Beth was and how Coach had called him an asshole. He wasn't mad but more confused."

"So, I need your help, man. I just won two trucks on auction on eBay for the business and we have to go down and pick them up. Hopefully you can go with me. They are matching route trucks"

"What's a Route Truck?"

"Like a delivery truck, a panel truck."

"I'm in" Mickey said, just glad to be talking about something that wasn't confrontational. "You mean next week?"

"Yeah" he said. Mickey asked as if he knew the answer "They're down in LA?

"No, Atlanta"

"Are you kidding me?

"I guess I should have led off with that. I'm figuring it's about five days and you could be back in time for grilling peaches on Saturday. I ran the directions on

Google and outside of a stretch from Atlanta to Memphis it's all one road – Interstate 40"

"Wow, I didn't see that coming. Have you ever bought trucks like this? What if they break down on the way? What if they don't start when we get there?

"The guy has a pretty good score – 100% on over 200 feedbacks! I'm feeling pretty good about that. He's driving them down from Greenville North Carolina, We fly in, check them out, get the keys and the pink slips and leave the next morning. Figure we fly down on Sunday and start driving on Monday morning."

"Road Trip!" they agreed and clashed their glasses together. They went inside, watched a little bit more of the game and never mentioned the ski meeting or the fight with Beth. It was a guy thing. They slid it down. Sliding it down meant that they weren't forgetting about it, just sliding it down till later when they could look it with a different perspective. They might talk about it on a ski lift next season or in the Jeep heading up the hill, but for now it was forgotten.

Ramshackled

"Sorry but pound is not a recognized entry. Please press the star button to..." Mickey hung up the phone with an anger that surprised even him. His assistant looked on in awe. "Shut up Jack. Don't even say a word". They went on, working for about five minutes, finishing up the days shoot. Mickey redialing, in earnest and concerned that all of his money was gone, "Kaput" as a German auto mechanic would say. The work was saved in digital files and being processed into a program that tightened up the images. Jack was putting the gear away during long downloads that could be eight minutes or longer. It was a well-run photography studio and the stands and lighting cases always went back in the same place.

"But you..." Jack was silenced by the rabbit in the head light eyes of his boss who commanded the moment with only a three inch rise of his forefinger and an off camera gaze. He was an able assistant whose own photography was original and well executed. He liked to photograph group scenes from different time periods. With the exchange between Mickey and the credit card company on speakerphone, he heard the whole exchange and it didn't look good for Mickey.

"Dame it" his fist came down hard on the desk and he starred into the computer screen in disbelief. . "How is that even remotely possible? There is no way that that account is closed out or wire transferred or whatever you said. But that's what you're telling me. Zero? Closed?"

"Yes Sir and thank you for being patient in this matter and please understand that we will look into this thoroughly. I will get back to you as soon as I have anything."

"Miss, I'm sorry, Lisa, is it? Yes, I appreciated you being thorough and everything but can you tell me what's happened here? How is it possible exactly?"

"Mr. McDaniel, according to our records, you came into our Broadway branch last Wednesday afternoon and closed the account. You also combined your travel account, joint savings, Christmas fund and college education funds into one savings account, which you closed on Friday. You then authorized the closure of your business checking account which closed all the accounts that were under the card. That is why your business checking was not available today when you were at the ATM in San Francisco. I am just reading this verbatim from the report. I know that this is frustrating, but that is what the paperwork says. The transactions were made at your local branch by tellers that you have had transactions many times and know you for years. The branch contacted me with details which they have on the video monitor system that shows your image making the exchanges. On one of the days you asked the manager about CD rates before you left"

After an appropriate silence he said "Thank you" and made sure he had her information. Mickey just sat there for the longest time, deflated indeed. Every dime he had except his IRA was in that string of accounts. "Dude, here is your paycheck". He said this into the monitor but loud enough for Jack to hear at the other end of the studio. About forty feet away by the roll up door, Jack stopped what he was doing. Unloading gear could wait. Jack was a toned muscular guy that went to the gym all the time. Lifting hundred pound cases was nothing. He turned towards Mickey and did a runway walk in his tight jeans and leather jacket. He was heavily tattooed, on his right side only, something that he had once tried to explain. His gate was lion like, smooth but not obvious. Mickey had stood up from his desk at the back of the studio was sitting on the corner of his desk, the check in both hands, looking straight ahead. Jack came up to him and stood closely, arms crossed.

Mickey held the check up higher and then moving his hands closer together, used his fingernails to rip it into two pieces. He then wadded it up into a ball and flicked it into his waste basket. "Two points. If you've been listening then you know that was a worthless piece of paper; garbage. I know you worked hard today and you know me, this isn't a run-down. I've still got these two credit cards in my pocket and I, well, I think they are still good. How about if we go and buy you two-hundred dollars of groceries and the store right now?"

Jack held his gaze for a time. "Yeah, that will work. I know what's going on here. It sounds like solid identity theft man. You've been marked good too!"

"Really, you've heard of this sort of thing man?" Jack relaxed a bit back into the wall, leaning against his right shoulder, hands in his jeans. "Not really, but I know a guy whose Dad lost some money on his credit card. But this is different man, sounds like a set up or something. This guy went into your bank, man. He must have been in disguise."

Mickey was grappling. Piecing it together, like a puzzle, step by step, he was listening and absorbing the magnitude. There was the "long term life savings" kind of magnitude and the earth shattering "what do I have in my wallet" kind of how will I pay the mortgage sort of thing. He switched back and forth in his head. "Yeah, he was in a disguise, man, a disguise of me."

"You sure have had some things lately Mickey. What's going on? Does this have anything to do with the thing at the church?" Jack never talked to him about it much, but had heard more from the rumor mill. He was Mickey's commercial photography assistant but not his wedding assistant. Mickey liked to have a woman assist him with the nuptials. It was hard enough being a male in a room full of women getting dressed and sometimes he would just send Katie in alone until everyone was ready. It was legendary in the wedding world and much talked about at the wedding associations and bridal fairs. Mickey caught a guy robbing his photography bag and all hell broke loose at a wedding. Jack hated weddings but liked Katie, who he believed was perfect for it, all bubbly and perky.

"It's possible I suppose. I don't know ...."

"So when's the big date?" Katie asked from the right side of the booth. The traffic was heavy at the Wedding Showcase, slated as the biggest show on the West Coast. There were hundreds of vendors ranging from the small single-guy flower shop to the national chain tuxedo company which came in on a freight carrier, diesel engines bellowing in the parking lot. At 7:45 am it was a nasty fray of wedding professionals jostling for room to unload their wares.

Mickey and Katie always got there early, staking out their 8 foot booth early so no one could grab six inches into their assigned booth space. The photos hung and albums spread out, Katie would stay behind as Mickey took the cart and boxes back to the truck and looked for parking. He would come back forty-five minutes later dressed in his black conservative suit with dark tie. In tow, would be the Sunday Chronicle, strong espresso lattes with triple shots and some pastry.

"May 23rd "would come the answer from the prospective client. Katie was great doing this, always with a smile that disarmed the bride. Sometimes they had their groom to be with them, usually walking with an exhausted gaze. They would have the look of someone at a car dealership with sticker shock. Often the mother would be with the bride.

When Mickey himself had gotten married it gave him unique insight into the other side of the project which he was unaware of. When his future mother-in-law came out for a wedding preparation weekend about six months before the big date an epiphany came over him like a wet sandwich. He had always believed in the healing power of humor and when there was so much stress it was an inevitable direction. Sitting on the couch one evening, the second night she was there, it occurred to him that his comedic approach was not well received, even by those that loved him, and accepted his odd and marginally inappropriate behavior. What hit him was a feeling that, in all those interviews he had, perhaps he had been a bit too flippant and not at all serious enough. Sitting there on the floor, stretching out his hamstrings, he saw the seriousness firsthand. They were mapping out their day starting with a trip to a bridal dress shop the next morning. They held in their laps brochures and paperwork. Mickey had decided, wisely, in the beginning to do whatever his young bride had wanted. But she kept asking him questions about what he preferred. "Do you think we should do salmon or off white?" His immediate response was "How about if we did both". In unison and one voice, his fiancé' and future mother-in-law said "No!" at the same time, syllable for syllable. Amanda continued on, as if to define her position, talking to Mickey but really talking to her mother. Whatever his answer was, hers was different. Trying to maintain separation was difficult but it was what he intended. However, before long he couldn't help become involved with an opinion here or an objection there. It was a thin line he walked, a wedding professional and all. But the abject intensity of a bride and her mother made him cringe. He thought of all the brides and mothers who had gone over his brochure the night before they would come to his studio. Were they this critical and detail oriented? Never again would he open with a joke or even lighthearted note. It changed his approach to interview meetings forever. And he had quite a number of these, in the evenings and on Sundays.

This was the heyday of our economy, the days that would be examined as the nexus of 'what went wrong'. There was so much business happening that one could hardly get into the city. The Bay Bridge was jammed with a hoard of commuters making their way into the land of commerce. It was this economy that drove his business and made him prosper from the art of photography. After all it wasn't these twenty-nine year olds that were paying for these lavish fifty to hundred-thousand dollar wedding events. However well employed and tightly connected, they didn't have the where-with-all or the depth in savings to pull of such events. It was Daddy. His house was appreciating $5K a month, so why not pull out some of that money that was just sitting there. And then there were the stock options and IPO's that falsely fueled false perceptions of wealth. Normal people became Day Traders on the stock market and teenagers had online trading accounts for birthday presents. There was a spending frenzy in this country, abject capitalism that ten years later would be viewed as irresponsibility.

At really good shows, ones that had good attendance he would find himself talking the sales talk hard, non-stop for hours on end. As soon as one potential client would leave with a smile, another would come up behind them, eager to talk about their wedding. Sometimes a bride would have her whole family in tow, maybe an aunt and often many bridesmaids. "Do you have packages?" "Do you use an assistant?", "Do you do video too?" Mickey would talk the talk sometimes feeling like his gums were flapping, but the longer he did it the better he became. "I am, simply, the best wedding photographer in the country". This would usually bring a smile from them as they could at least appreciate his marketing acumen.

Towards the end of the show an Asian couple approached him and asked if he could shoot their small wedding on a Thursday in a few weeks. Andy and his young bride to be, Anita, stood very close together, touching at all times, perhaps for support. Anita seemed nervous and Andy was her rock. Mickey always jumped on a mid-week wedding as they were a rarified bird. Unlike destination resorts like Hawaii that have weddings every day of the week, there were few that came his way. A photographer in Maui could shoot constantly with the influx of Japanese Yen looking for a destination wedding on the cheap. Compared to Japan, there were deals to be found out in the Pacific, so much that with the money they saved, they could buy airfare for their guests.

"So where are we having this lovely affair?" he queried. They both came up to his shoulder and he found himself leaning over as to not make the height difference apparent. "Yes, we are having a ceremony at the Saint Peter and Paul's Church" she said softly. "But we only need you for the ceremony for an hour and then some family photos on the steps of the church" chimed in Andy, making sure that he knew they were not looking for one of the big packages on the brochure he was holding in his hand. "Can you do just one hour?"

"Well, if you were standing here talking to me about a Saturday wedding the answer would be no. But I'm always looking for some shoots during the week and they aren't as competitively priced. So, yes, we would love to shoot your Thursday wedding and I'm sure it will be lovely. Do you know that Joe DiMaggio and

Marilyn Monroe got married at that church in North Beach?"

"No" they both said with a smile. Mickey didn't think they really knew who he was talking about. After getting their information and promising to call in a few days he said goodbye and they all seemed like friends. He was glad to get the little job, making him feel like he had somewhat paid for the show with one little job. Sometimes it would be hard to gage the success of a bridal faire. Brides might call you next week or next year and there were no guarantees.

Breaking down the booth with a solid sale and money in his pocket for this month, made him cheery. At exactly 4pm the show erupted in a breakdown frenzy that always amused him. It was like an Indian encampment being struck so the tribe could move on to hunt the buffalo. Civility was set aside as all the vendors vied for parking spots to load up their vehicles. The courtesy and respect that had earmarked the day gave way to a herd mentality in a mass exodus. Like thirsty boar heading for the only watering hole for miles, there was honking of horns and rudeness. It was all part of the long day that he had paid dearly for and hoped to be profitable.

Andy's wedding ceremony was at 1pm and Mickey made sure he got into the city early just in case the traffic would be a problem. He would always prefer to be there early and grab a coffee and the newspaper instead of stressing on the Bay Bridge that he was late.

Like many weddings this day was not simple and straight forward. Andy and Anita decided to pay for some extra coverage so Mickey met them at the hotel room downtown. He approached every job with best absolute attitude that he could and this was not an exception. However, it was just himself. They weren't paying extra for an assistant and Katie was in school anyway. So he went just a little bit lighter than usual; two systems instead of three, but he was used to working this way.

Immersion into a smallish Victorian room full of bridesmaids and a bride didn't ruffle his feathers; he got in, got what he needed and got out. The bride's mother was speaking Mandarin and so there was constant banter back and forth as the Mom seemed to be bossing her around. That got most of the four bridesmaids talking Mandarin as well. Mickey moved amongst the rhetoric with the innocence of a school boy with an eye of a pirate. If they only knew what he was thinking and how dastardly he could be. He was mostly ignored and lightly tolerated. Being a fly on the wall suited him. He wasn't after portraiture at this part of the coverage and only wanted the realness that the event offered in spite of itself.

During one particularly heated exchange between the Bride and her Sister, the Mother started screaming at them both and Mickey caught the gaze of a lovely

Bridesmaid in the mirror. She was young and sharp looking and amused by the goings on. It was a brief look shared that assured him he was not losing it and as no one had talked to him yet it was a good assurance. There is always something that goes awry with every wedding and it usually happens here. The bride can't get into her dress or there is a button missing; perhaps the flowers or the makeup lady is late arriving. Today's issue was the Bride's daughter, out of position for the ceremony and stuck in traffic on the other side of town. This he got in the hallway from the women in the mirror. She continued to find the situation amusing but not out of the ordinary, knowing the Bride.

Running through Mickey's old fashioned mind was the thought of who the father was, but he dismissed this. It had to be Andy's daughter.

"NO, I don't care. We will just have to wait for her to get here. I'm not going down the aisle without my daughter there, my flower Girl" said Anita in unexpected English with an accent. The mother fired back something in Mandarin, the meaning obvious. Her words hung there stale in the rooms still air for just a moment. Then all the females started talking at the same time, vigorously in their native tongue.

Mickey manufactured the only portrait he really sought, that of mother and daughter. He got them together by the window - a lovely natural light setting saying "thank you" about eight times nervously. He continued taking candid shots of the primping and dressing. He moved amongst the half dressed women with the acceptance of a priest or a doctor, given a one day pass to see women in their bras and slips, adjusting their breasts or sliding stockings evenly over their pale flesh. "I've got everything I need Anita! I'll see you over at Saint Mary's."

"Thank you Mickey" was the soft reply from the Bride. As he left the room he noticed a quiet calm had descended upon the women. There were no cell phone calls now and no screaming between parent and the soon to be wed. It was an uneven calm that Mickey left, closing the door and heading downstairs.

The rooms at the Fairmont were so small he thought as he went down the carpeted hallway past many more rooms. He had done a job in the Presidential Suite once and it was a rambling rooftop compound bigger than many homes, but the little rooms on the eighth floor were built for simpler times and smaller people. The Rolling Stones stayed in the rooftop suite when they were in town as well as every president since Roosevelt. Clinton had snubbed the hotel by staying across the street at the Mark Hopkins. He was such a street fighting man.

Mickey made his way to his truck, parked in the basement below; a cave of a garage that needed careful navigation. Heading towards Chinatown, he was trying to envision a parking space opening up for him in the next few minutes and found something not so far from the Church.

Time for a quick stop in the McDonalds felt like a break on a tour through an Asian city. Ninety percent of the people inside were Asian and all the ladies behind the counter spoke in fluent Mandarin with no English heard at all. The items on the board had Chinese script and American prices. But his burger and fries tasted the same.

His first duty was to make sure he had access to the choir loft. Finding Father Brian took longer than normal as it was not a weekend and when Mickey found him in was in a bad mood. "It's locked up and you can't use it" he barked in an unreligious tone. Mickey knew that he had to tread carefully as this was always the case with Father Brian. "Oh Please! Can't we open it? When I sold my service to Andy, he and his lady fell in love with the choir loft shot during the ceremony. Is there anything we can do? They just love your church so much and it would mean the world to them." That was his best approach with Father Brian and he had buttered him up all he could. "I'll try and find the key" He waddled away with his short steps down the aisle towards the sacristy and Mickey could only watch.

He set up his light and camera gear and waited patiently. Before long the small wedding party showed with parents and relatives gathering in the front of the church. The flowers were being set up, the key arrived for the choir loft and everything was proceeding as planned.

Inside the church, he found a row in the back to store his gear that was out of the way but accessible. Even though he was traveling light, he was always amazed by the amount of gear it took to photograph a simple event. But when that "simple" event is so time constrained and your assignment is to capture memories that will last a lifetime, there is heightened concentration. And this required him to bring backups of everything he had, camera bodies, and lens for every shot he would take. Equipment could always breakdown, but your job as a professional was not to miss the shots because of it. So, he stood there, leaning over his camera case, checking and double checking the gear.

Hearing the clamor of groom's men in the vestibule he headed that way, arriving just at the moment that Andy's mother was pinning a flower on his solid black tux. A special moment to be sure and one of the classics, Mickey glided in to retrieve the shot with the quiet eloquence of a cat. Andy smiled seeing him. "How are the ladies?" he wanted to know. "Are they heading this way now?" Mickey nodded that he thought so "yes", but playing it cool he didn't mention the traffic estranged daughter caught in the South Bay. It might not have been his child after all and maybe there was some issue involved that was not his place to bring up. Mickey just kept it lighthearted and when his mother was finished putting his corsage on, he got a lovely portrait of the two of them up against the stained glass window. He motioned for the father to join them and then did some shots of Andy's family, together in the front of the church.

Like all good bride and grooms they didn't want to see each other before the ceremony, something about bad luck. So, Andy was shuffled off to the side of the church when Anita arrived with her party. It was one of Mickey's favorite photo opportunities and he pursued it with many images. Anita was whisked into a small "getting ready room" to the left where she waited with her ladies and her mother. It was there that she announced she wasn't going down the aisle until her daughter arrived which got everyone nervous right off and you could cut the tension in the room with a bread knife. No one said anything and Anita just looked at the floor.

The ceremony was slated to begin at 11am. Mickey went to the priest's area where Andy and his two Grooms Men were sequestered and in waiting. He noticed that the priest was not one of his favorites, a small square shaped man who walked with a distinctive waddle, one leg being shorter than the other. Adorned in his full length pastoral robe he moved slowly and side to side, like a penguin. He was kind of a mean old man. The first wedding Mickey did in Saint Mary's was with him he yelled at the Groomsmen for parking in the white zone in front of the church and threatened to call the police if they didn't move their cars. He was not a happy man.

It was not his place to announce things as he was more of a fly on the wall photographer just capturing the goings on. But, as it was just about eleven he felt inclined to update his client on the proceedings. "Hi Andy- You look great. Hey guys. So Anita wanted me to tell you that your daughter isn't here yet and she wants to wait for her." Before Andy had time to respond, the priest who's back was to them as he put on his colorful Mass Robes, said " No! No waiting." Mickey didn't want to engage him at all and just looked at Andy who motioned him to follow him to the hall. "Where is she Mick?" With calm he explained that she was on her way but that they were tied up in traffic. The little girl had spent the night with Anita's older sister who had, apparently, somewhat of a reputation for drama.

Mickey went back to the ladies waiting room with news that the priest had another meeting before noon and had said that he wouldn't "wait around all day" for her. "Wow, he sounds like a jerk" said one of the Bridesmaids. Anita grew more determined and could only grit her teeth while looking at the Italian marble on the floor.

It was becoming clear to Mickey that both sides here were rooted in stubbornness and were about to butt heads. He kept going back and forth between the two rooms, trying to keep everyone informed. On his fourth trip to the priests room, the time clicking to 11:15 now, the priest said he was heading out to the altar and "we will either do this thing or not." Mickey thought he was being a bit harsh about it and against his better judgment, volunteered to go once again to the bride's room and let her know.

When he opened the door on the left side of the altar he passed a huge pulpit with winding stairs. It wasn't used anymore but you could just feel the sermons of old being delivered with tremendous enthusiasm. Passing the first row of pews he could feel everyone's gaze upon him as if HE knew what was going on. Their patience was waning now in the twentieth minute of delay.

"The Priests says we have to go now or he's going to leave!" he said quickly when he entered the brides room. "He says he has someplace else to go. Don't shoot the messenger okay, he just told me to tell you that." The women erupted once again in high pitched dialog that was hard on the ears. The bridesmaid from the hallway shook her head and softly said the she wasn't going to do it.

Mickey had no choice now, but to head back to the priest. His shoes went "clackety, clack" as walked quickly down the hard tile floor. As he entered the small door to the left of the altar, the priest was there, moving quickly, almost running him over. He just looked at Mickey "It doesn't matter. I know what she said. It doesn't matter. I'm going out there to address the good people and this thing is either going forward or it is over." Mickey literally pressed himself against the wall as the priest's robe rubbed against his photographers vest.

The priest took his position at the altar but didn't say anything. He was reading his Bible and not looking up.

Mickey went back to the brides room, confused thoroughly now, truly a messenger. "The Priest is up there now and he wants to see you." She looked at him ashen white but said nothing. The Bridesmaids were all on their phones, talking to who he knew not. It was very quiet. "She's not answering her cell phone. What should we do?" No one knew what do and no one was talking. Mickey wished for simpler times but reminded himself he was getting paid well but that didn't help much. The Bride was sitting down with all her ladies standing. She motioned towards her photographer and he came to her side. She whispered "Tell him five minutes. If she's not here in five minutes then we will do it."

Mickey felt this was getting somewhere and walked towards the altar with renewed enthusiasm. He could see Andy his men over on the right side looking bedeviled. Heading straight for the Priest, he got close and whispered the Brides request. He grunted, shut his Bible and was going to quit when the front doors leading onto Broadway burst open and even through the glare of the hot sun burning through the doorway both Mickey and the priest could see a little five year old running towards the Brides room with two adults chasing her. There were sounds of relief issued in multiple languages with the joy and relief. The Priest settled back to the pulpit with Andy and his men shuffling back and forth, knowing that it was a go.

Mickey hustled back to the Brides room to get that photo of Mother and Daughter long overdue. Everyone was smiling. Even Mom was grinning ear to ear and very content. Mickey went to work capturing the Bridal Party as they poured out of the tiny room into the lobby. They got in line quickly, the little girl leading the way after Mom and Dad were escorted in. Mickey moved to the front of the altar and got a shot of the men looking towards the door. They were lined up in a row, their shoulders back, standing tall.

As the Bride entered the church and those in attendance stood up to honor her walk down the aisle, the moment came into itself. The frustrations of the last half hour melted into an embrace of the now and there was a wonder to it. Everyone's face showed the beauty present in the actions of this young couple that had planned and scheduled the late morning wedding on paper and in their heads.

Mickey knew all too well the Catholic ceremony and could follow it in his head. It was a break for the photographer really as there were only a few shots during the ceremony. He shot a Korean wedding once that was in Korean but was Catholic. He could even pick out the cadence in the Lord's Prayer and could fill in the blanks. When the Korean Priest said "Howry, Howry, Howry" he knew it was over and it was time to jump into action and capture the kiss.

Andy & Anita's wedding day had all come into focus, the early morning fog had yielded to blue sky when they walked out the church doors and held a little reception on the steps. There were many hugs and some tears. Everyone smiled for the photos.

Mickey motioned to the Bride that she had to do some formal photographs at the altar and that the Priest was gone. "I know they usually wait around for a photo opportunity, but we were a little late out of the gate. But hey, we got lots of shots with him in it. But let's go in, eh" he beckoned her with his hand.

Mickey usually left his gear bags in the last aisle of the pews. As it was such a small wedding he put the bags about half way down the aisle. As it was just an hour coverage he didn't have Katie helping and watching things. With the nuptials complete, the bride and groom went to the altar for family shots. Mickey was about fifteen feet in front of them taking photos of six sets of parents as the couple's family had both gone thru divorce and remarried. This was sometimes challenging but usually it was all smiles and cooperation. As Mickey was arranging the bride's same sex partners on the left side, Andy pointed behind the photographer- "Hey Mickey! Is that your stuff? Is that guy taking your stuff?" Mickey turned around to see the back of a thief heading towards the street with both of his gear bags which contained an extra body and a number of lenses. "Hey" he shouted, putting down the medium format camera he was working with. "Hey, what do you think you are doing there" and he ran down the aisle after him. He was running with the fear of stolen gear in his head which gave him courage beyond his means. The large Asian male kept walking towards the door and Mickey was just about to grab him. In a decisive moment Mickey realized that he had to leap towards him and in that same moment the thief turned. He had both bags in his left hand. His right hand came across his body and a heavy gage chain thrust towards Mickey. Instinctually he put his left hand up to stop it, hoping he might grab it and make it useless to the thief. But it was too heavy and was swung with great speed.

With a slap it hit Mickey's wrist bone and he knew it was broken. But he hadn't caught the end of the chain which snapped back and hit him right below the eye. Mickey dropped to his knees and the thief was gone out the door and onto the steps of the great church. And just like that and in a matter of seconds, it was over. The end of the chain had missed his eye by inches and a welt was already growing on his upper check.

Andy was in shock but made his way to Mickey, helping him to his feet as they heard the getaway car squeal out of park. "Wow! Are you okay? I can't believe that happened here in this church like that." The bride's father was on the phone to 911 but it was too late. All his lenses and backup gear were gone. Father Brian appeared out of nowhere and used some holy water on Mickey's check bone saying it was miracle he wasn't more seriously hurt. Paramedics arrived and put a bandage on his check and a splint on his broken wrist. Being the professional he was Mickey got up and took the rest of photos which only lasted around ten minutes and everyone was pleased with this.

Within three or four minutes police were on the scene. Mickey was surrounded by the concerned Bridal Party but still couldn't get to his feet and was just sitting on the floor now. "that chain could have killed you dude. You are lucky!" But right now, at this moment he didn't feel too lucky. But he did have all the day's images in his pocket. He could replace that camera but the images of the ceremony could never be replaced. Good thing he attended that photography meeting where this was suggested.

Officer Daniels arrived with a paramedic right behind him. "Let's get a look at the hand young man. I understand there was a chain that you were hit with" Mickey went on to explain it the best he could. He started to be very glad he wasn't hit in the head. The paramedic wanted to get him to the hospital right away. "Can you just wrap it up so I can finish taking some photographs here? I don't have an assistant today and don't want to leave these good folks hanging." Debra the paramedic was shaking her head back and forth and holding his hand in her grasp. "Does it hurt here? How about this? Can you make a fist?" Mickey tried but there was surprisingly little response although he could feel everything. Mickey rose to his feet as the bridal party clapped and cheered him like a ballplayer. Looking at Debra with determination "Just tape it up okay. And then I'll go to the hospital. I promise." She agreed and had some paperwork for him to sign, although his signature didn't look too good. The police weren't so easy and demanded that he deal directly with the police report. Mickey went over to one of the pews and sat down with Officer Daniels to his side, asking him a barrage of questions. There were timeline questions and questions like did he ever see this guy before? Did he get a clear view of his face? "All I saw was the chain, coming my way." There were insurance questions. Mickey described the getaway car as a late model sedan that was tan or brown in color. After about fifteen minutes the interview concluded and Mickey turned his attention to the wedding. He only needed about fifteen minutes worth of shooting and he could feel good about honoring his commitment and delivering for his client.

Mickey ambled up to the altar to the waiting wedding party. Resting the bottom of his camera on his lower left arm, quite a bit up from his wrist, he was able to steady the shot and click the button with his left hand. This was awkward as the button is on the left hand side, but he was able to make it work. Feeling a need to move things along he asked everyone for their attention to which they responded. He got the family shots done in five minutes. He spent another five minutes with the Bride & Groom and promised that he would do a little portrait of them when they picked up their photos. Andy slipped him a hundred dollar bill and told him "you are the man, Mickey."

It took forever to heal that wrist but at least it wasn't his shooting arm. The confrontation lingered and there were a few nightmares but as the priest had said, it could have been worse.

Thankful

Today of all days, he has to see the Ex. Her eyes would immediately case him toe to head with piercing glaze. There it would fix for some time until Mickey looked down as he was always the first to look away. He wasn't afraid of direct eye contact, but it was just that his ex-wife had a power over him that was unworldly.

A Chautauqua, that was what Persig called it when he went on the road with his son in Motorcycle Maintenance to get his Zen out and showed his boy how different life could be,. Outside of his son's house, he once tried to explain, "There is a world that is different from your usual day to day with some things you can't possibly imagine."

"Why would I want different "Jay had said that morning on his way to school.

"Well, first off, you wouldn't be going to pre-school right now and after that I wouldn't have to go to work and make money. You go to work for a couple of years and then talk to me"

Mickey thought that he needed to get away. Coach needed him to go and he agreed. Why not wrap Jay into the equation. Mickey had wanted to do something like that last year but there was never the time, between his scheduled shoots and the money which seemed to be there and then disappeared. And then so did the time.

The Ex opened the door like Beowulf at the gates of a castle. There were those eyes and they had steel in them. As she leaned up against the door jam, Jay ran underneath saying "See ya Mom." Turning to Mickey, Amanda said with softness "Thanks Mickey, you two have fun okay. Do you have everything Jayee?" She always prolonged the end of his name lovingly. When she said his name it had an ascorbic edge to it that always gave him pause. Mickey liked walking his son to school and felt like a kid himself sometimes.

Jay's eyes lit up like headlights when he saw him, greeting him with a hug and a smile. He loved ridding in the big root-beer brown Plymouth and called it the motorboat. "How did it go young man?" Mickey said the way he always did. "Aw Dad, you know".

Usually he would ask "Tell me about your day….what was the best thing that happened today" he said looking for some kind of revelation that the nuns had imparted. "The best thing was….ah….I know….when Jimmy pulled on Loretta's pony tail and she screamed forever. It was super loud and the nuns freaked…"

With Jay letting himself in the front seat of the big Plymouth, Amanda continued looking at him without blinking it seemed. "So, I have this idea I need you to consider, Ok?" She spun around and just stared blankly at him, waiting. This look stopped him cold and he thought she looked like runway model. He knew for an instant that he still loved her, and that he would always love her. He couldn't think of what to say now and just looked at her admiringly so. The Ex, didn't really pick up on that and thought he was giving her a little attitude about something. Slowly he began to tell her his idea and her face was blank, no tells and Mickey had no idea what she was thinking just then.

"What? So how much do you need?" Ex wanted to know the damage right off. He had at times borrowed some money from her. She had a good job, something that Mickey was unfamiliar with. But it had been some time now that he had to borrow money, although he totally half-expected that response from her. Mickey had never had a job. Most people found that impossible to believe, but the man never actually worked for anyone in his life. As a teenager he started to trim neighbor's trees. His Dad bought him a Ford 350 flatbed one year as a present and that was all the encouragement that he needed. Not only could he cut the trees down now, but he could take them to the dump and get rid of them. He was in business as a tree guy. He learned how to climb them and raise the canopy. His summers were consumed with as much work as could do, with all the neighbors bragging about such a fine job he did. So he never got one of those summer jobs – he just cut down trees. When he was in college, whenever he needed money he would just climb up a tree for somebody and away it went. When he got out of college, when everyone else was in management training programs he put a little classified ad in the paper and got five calls the first day. And he rode the tree cutting as far as he could, until his body got tired of climbing trees and he pursued his photography more and more. He could always reach back for some emergency money in the early days by doing some tree work, but it became less and less.

"No it's not like that girl" Mickey pleaded for sympathy. "I don't need any of your money I just want to have this time with Jay before he is so big that he wants to ignore me. I'm actually going to make money on the trip- a grand at least"

She quietly said "Well I guess it would be okay. I'm working on a project all next week at the office and could use the time to get serious."

"How long would he be gone – when would you two be back" Ex was thinking.

"I have to be back to grill peaches on Saturday. We leave on Sunday, start driving on Monday morning and should roll in on Friday afternoon. Coach mapped it out on Google, and has the trip down to a science."

"What exactly are you two doing again?" the mother in her had to know.

"He bought two trucks for his business from a company in Greenfield South Carolina. The guy is driving them down to Atlanta and we will meet him and the trucks there at the hotel Sunday night. They are big delivery trucks. We leave early Monday morning and plan on driving eight hours a day. There's got to be a pool at every hotel – that's one of our rules. So, it will be fun. Plus Jay and I will get a chance to be together in a special way"

"Sounds like you've got a plan and that's all good……..ok, but you be careful. I want calls every evening. And emails..."

They never actually divorced and might not in the future. Their friends were in disbelief of this and encouraged some finality. But Mickey and Amanda didn't seem to need it.

Last Thanksgiving, at Jay's request, Mickey attended her family's Thanksgiving dinner. He wondered how exactly that was going to unfold. He was busy with work and a couple of side things came up and suddenly he was in Thanksgiving week and there was now no backing out. Mickey didn't like the holidays anymore, especially Thanksgiving and Christmas because it reminded him of his family and what he had lost.

The women were in the kitchen and the guys were watching football with drinks in hand. Mickey could take only so much of this domestic harmony with a Rockwellian twist. He went into the kitchen, hearing them talking and laughing as he went thru the dining room. Yes, he thought, this would be a welcomed change. Maybe someone would tell a story and there would most certainly be laughs and cheers. The minute he walked in the swinging door they stopped talking. The giggling laughs lingered for a moment but as Mickey pulled his head out of the fridge and looked around, there was nothing. The women got very busy checking the stuffing, the beans and of course the temperature of the turkey. Mickey opened the beer he had just pulled out and leaned up against the counter. Almost immediately her Mom needed that particular piece of counter space, so he moved. He awkwardly turned towards the door without uttering a word.

Not wanting to sit down with the guys again, he walked towards the backyard, not really meaning to go outside. He passed an opened door which was the bedroom of Amanda's Grandmother. Amanda had talked about her health problems but Mickey only remembered her from the wedding. She had a boyfriend then. Phillip was his name and he was into dancing. At the wedding they hardly stopped dancing, even dancing slowly when the band wasn't playing. That was before the Alzheimer's kicked in and slowed her down considerably. There was talk in the family about how long she had dementia and references were made to things that happened decades ago. Maybe what she did way back then was at the root of what engaged her so negatively now.

She was in her chair with legs propped up and she had the palsy in her arms. She had her head back and her mouth half open. For a second, Mickey thought she had just died. Then he saw her fragile chest move about an eighth of an inch as she took a breath. Her arms were crossed and she breathed heavily thru her mouth, even though the oxygen which ran all the time was running a stream thru the nose. There was a snoring sounded desperate and exacerbated in need of oxygen. She made little grunts and moans. The moans were an expression of tiredness. Mickey remembered the most tired he had ever been, after being up for almost two days on the road and how he let out a groan to end all groans when he hit the bed with his head.

The last time he was in this house, an occasion he couldn't exactly remember, he had paused at this same door jam and watched her as she sat in her chair. She was not so far along that time, but he was struck by the emptiness he had seen. She was shaking then and saying 'oh no, oh no over and over like a mantra to keep her calm. The TV was on but the image was snow. She held the remote in her hand, but he wasn't sure if she was really moving the buttons but the station wasn't changing and the snow reminded him of the image on his folk's old tube that was powered by antenna. What stuck him was how she stared at the screen as if she was seeing something there. She was living in an abstract world of the past and having conversations in her mind with friends long lost or deceased. She was living on the other side more than not, crossing over to the other side in mind not yet in body. Besides the aggravated state, she was content, in no pain and non-threatened

A string of fate tied them all together, and it was if Mickey was seeing this for the first time now. He would be there when Amanda's mother died, they would both be at Jay's graduation from college and support him in whatever he chose to pursue, Jay would take care of them both when they were old. And all this sprouted from a night of passion back when they were younger. That time of innocence ironically turned into a lifetime of intertwined fate and connectivity

Made in the USA
Charleston, SC
03 March 2013